A Novel

Songs
from a Voice,

Being the Recollections, Stanzas,
and Observations of Abe Runyan,
Song Writer and Performer

Baron Wormser

woodhall press
NORWALK, CT

Woodhall Press
81 Old Saugatuck Road, Norwalk, Connecticut, 06855
Woodhallpress.com

Distributed by INGRAM

Text design: Casey Shain
Proofer: Theresa Pelicano
Copyeditor: Paulette Baker

Library of Congress Cataloging-in-Publication Data available
ISBN 978-1-949116-12-0 (paperback)
ISBN 978-1-949116-13-7 (ebook)

First Edition

For Janet

"Imagination is what you had and maybe all you had."
—Bob Dylan, Interview in *Dylan on Dylan*

"And the inner impulse of this effort and operation, what induced it?"
—Robert Browning, "Introductory Essay" from *Letters of Percy Bysshe Shelley*

A Note to the Reader

This book evokes the circumstances of an imagination. The terrain of this imagination hearkens to Bob Dylan, but I have invented a character, Abe Runyan, who is very much a fiction. There are correspondences as to where Abe comes from and where he goes; he traces Dylan's roots and early arc. No one knows, however, where, ultimately, an imagination comes from. Abe is like Bob—Jewish, a Midwesterner—but Abe exists wholly in words, and that is the point of him: to aim in that ever improbable direction, to vindicate the promptings of imagination, to salute the importance of what came from seemingly nowhere. Inwardness mocks the externals of biography, but fiction may trace a finer line, how one renamed life deserves another.

I met a snake one day while I was walking home from school. I was hiding out under the usual bushel basket of doubt, wondering where my way was, lost in proud clouds I couldn't tell anyone about, when this snake crossed my path, then stopped and said, "You've heard of me, Abe, from various hustles I've run and how the human race got undone, and some of that's true and some's not, but I get around town and now I'm down with you."

Nothing, no one under the ever-sun was going to upstart me. No freak-out on my part. I was too out of it to drop my heart because a snake started talking. I lived in "could be" already. "Well, whatever you've got to say to me, I've heard it already. I may be a kid, but I'm a mighty Yid. I can rant and gallivant."

"Enough," said the snake. "I get that you are big on yourself, which is nothing new with your kind—blind human mind, groping and hoping and, as they say, these self-pleased days, coping. No need to lay your trip and schtick on me. I was winding around the bower and making people cower before you ever descended from your intellectual tower. My abode is the crossroad where the soul gets sold." Here the snake rose up a bit as if to strike. "Don't worry, Abe. I'm not going to hurt you the way you think I might. I've got better griefs to inflict, ones that make you sick when you feel well, ones that get under your skin so your flesh feels like it's within and your thoughts peel off you."

I didn't like the sound of that and said I had to go. I was up for anything but not everything.

"Not so fast, hombre," the snake declared. "I came along to make you aware. If that scares you then you'll never share what's in you with others. You'll just mutter and stutter and hang your head like you already were dead like a lot of the human disgrace." The snake eyed me. "Don't think about doing something violent. That would *be stupid. If you pick up a rock, you're even more doomed. You'll be stuck for life in your low-hope room, your head an angry tomb."*

What kind of time could I have stalled for? And I had to admit he made me curious. I liked things to happen that I couldn't tell anyone about, that made me feel special but that made me feel secret, too, like I was invisible in public, like no one ever could guess me or suggest to me or wrongheadedly bless me. Still, this character had danger emblazoned all over him. He was bound to know more than I did. Didn't he invent sin?

"What if I offered you a deal?" the snake asked. His voice was a seductive hiss like he knew he couldn't miss. An ancient carny, he knew an easy mark.

"No deals," I said. "With me it's all or nothing. I don't want your sympathy or your reparation treaty or your drizzle of metaphysical iced tea. Do I make myself clear?"

"I expect this folderol. It goes with my job. You deal with human-kind and you're going to get a lot of their fast-talking rot. Words are a big conceit. People in their verbal steeples don't grasp how the other creatures know something too. No offense meant that you weren't born a wren or a snake or a horse."

"You mean—"

"I didn't come here to duel with a fool. I've noticed your tendency to inner photography. You're going to need sustenance—not snake meat but something more complete."

"Riddles get me down, man. Could you come out straight and say it?"

"I've got a guitar. Six strings that ping, ring, and sing." I started to feel lost. My head started to swim like I didn't know where to end or begin, like I was living in something that couldn't happen but did. My tongue felt tossed, my eyes crossed. I wasn't going to cry. I was never

going to cry, but I thought of my grandma and how she sighed, how her sad ocean leaked out, and I knew what that was about even though I hadn't seen where she'd been.

"Everyone has a guitar, kid. They sing what's already been sung. They inhabit the days and offer their out-of-tune praise. But there's more to be felt and voiced."

"Why do you care?" My wits were coming back. I could see through the crack in the sky inside me.

"Fairy tales don't come true, Abe. I know that better than anyone, but old stories have and do. You're one of the old ones yourself, walking down this street, heading home from school, wondering and mooning and tuning the universe in your head: what could be, should be, would be. A real circus upstairs."

"Who cares?" It came out more desperate than flip. "Got a ciggie?"

"Snakes don't smoke, don't tell bad jokes, and don't unnecessarily emote. Here's the upshot, kid. You're going to have a chance, but you can't trust anyone. You're going to be on your own. What you're seeing right now is a vision. And that's going to be who you are."

"And how can you, Mr. Snake Vision, tell me who I am?" I pulled out a Marlboro, waved it in the sonic air.

"I'm impossible and improbable, Abe. That means you're done for but unaccounted for. Good luck in the dream world."

He didn't disappear because he never was there. I made stuff up routinely. Or stuff made me up: Abe walked home from school, his head flaky, snaky, un-wide-awake, full of the mistaken and half-baked, but cocky nonetheless, like he had the inside track on some strange success. Like he knew something no one else knew. Like what he thought was true.

. . .

The vanquished nights were dark and cold—
Words froze in brittle air—
I looked for light in the silent sky—
My heart so unaware.

The piled snows—snow way above a child's head—muffled all sound, but I heard the cold mutter, whistle and creak, below-zero and well below-zero, not human weather, a blue-black grip, a grasping wraith, a void that probed your every pore. I feared I would be cold forever, my fingers unbending, my precious ears hard as plates. "There goes Abe, the Abominable Snowboy. Walks like he's made of petrified wood." I did not want to leave my bed or house on those northern winter mornings. I burrowed under my Hudson Bay blanket and imagined staying there, cocooned. Some glad day the dark months would go away. I pictured myself outside, wearing a T-shirt, riding my Schwinn, happily sweating, delirious with summer. Then my mom would come in and yank the covers. "Get up," she'd bark. Sometimes she'd philosophize: "Time waits for no man and especially not for a boy." I'd sigh—to preserve self-respect—then very quickly dress.

Outside, the sun lied. I'd stand on the playground at noon in January while the sun lolled in a clear sky, a happy stupid circle like what I drew in the half hour my teacher called "art," but with no warmth for me, the dumb sum of sweaters, mittens, and a felted cap that weighed at least three pounds. A wonder—as my grandma would have said—my head didn't fall off. Yet there was the sun, mighty and feeble. I knew about the seasons and people talking, how winters weren't as cold and summers weren't as hot, how the world was running down. I didn't believe that talk. The way the cold knifed through me, I might as well have been wearing paper. I heard the stories about people freezing to death, people who got lost in the woods or fell through the ice. "Did you hear about Len Olsen?"

My chief hobby, beyond stamp collecting and in the good weather chucking a rubber ball against the side of the house, was overhearing. If you asked me what I've been doing for a lifetime, I'd say not singing or writing or playing the guitar but "listening in." Every child begins in that curious place, learning that the world around you isn't for you, though you are bound to act as though it is. You crawl then you totter then you walk with your hands outstretched, touching, touching, then clutching. But right from the beginning you can hear. That seems why you are lying in that crib. No one comprehends your cries, but you hear the cackles, lullabies, shrieks, and cajoling clucks. The words everyone exchanges are so much babble, but you hear the tones. They speak. They become you.

I've stayed there with the sounds, not forgetting anything I've heard, hoarding it: the train whistle from the tracks two blocks from our house, my mother scolding me, my father's fatalist mottoes, the back door slamming, the mop swishing along the kitchen floor, the steam banging in the radiators on those frozen mornings. And, best of all, music, how sometimes my mother would hum or sing while she cleaned, ironed, cooked, baked, and a dozen other tasks; how some-times, if I asked, she would teach me the song then and there, popular songs like "The Tennessee Waltz," which was recent but sounded old. I liked its lilt and sway. The words seemed to put my mother into that dreamy, faraway place she liked to go. The song was sad—an old friend stealing her sweetheart—but for my mother, that seemed to make it better.

No one ever knows how deep a song can go. There can never be enough songs, yet one can be plenty. My mother would disappear, there in front of me but not there. She and her song scared but pleased me.

If you go about bent on hearing and overhearing, you can lose yourself; or maybe, to begin with, you don't care about yourself in the way that people act possessive: my life, my hat, my Davy Crockett lunchbox. Sure, I brought my books to school, not someone else's, but over decades I've done my share of borrowing, notes and words, those filaments of sound that are there for the taking. One tune is bound to become another. Music really is in the air.

There's plenty I wish I'd never heard, but it's not like you can put your head under a pillow so the hard stuff doesn't get to you. There were whispers in our house because families create whispers the way spiders create webs. The main location of whispers was behind my parents' bedroom door. That's the basic source of mysteries, the lives of the king and queen, but my mother whispered to my grandmother; my sister and I whispered about whatever we didn't want our parents to know about; and my grandmother employed a stage whisper, not really a whisper but pretending to be a whisper, when she wanted to make some point that she shouldn't say but was going to say anyway. "Excuse me," she would say by way of beginning. I could feel my parents brace themselves.

The whispers in my house weren't anything amazing—no child had been given up for adoption. They still were whispers, though—the can't-say-but-have-to-say about other lives, daily hassles, never enough dough, random doubts—and they filtered into me the way whispers do, a sift of uncertainty and secrecy, of more than can be said out loud. One of the blessings of songs is that they puncture whispers. The fog of nervous feeling or what feels like unbearable knowledge lifts. Whatever was under wraps doesn't have to be.

There were five of us in the house in which I grew up—my parents, Max and Susan; my sister, Karen; my father's mother, Reva; and myself. No one song could tell you every aspect and angle of what each of us felt day by day and how we acted when we were together. You could say that wasn't a song's job, but a song could give the complications their due. The situations—Reva had a stockpile of grievances, for instance—bounced off the walls like so many psychological tennis balls. We weren't the "Tennessee Waltz," more like the "Throbbing Jewish Two-Step." I overheard, I lived in those drafty rooms, and eventually I sang.

* * *

I heard a voice like the end of time—
Cut from the cloth of fear—
Then someone laughed, someone sang—
As if we could live here.

Part of what I overheard was never there. I mean about my uncle who died in the war. I was little, and don't remember him. My dad had something wrong with his eyes, so he didn't go fight but my uncle did. He was in the infantry in Europe. There must have been a moment when the telegram came or someone came to the door and announced that my uncle was "missing in action." There must have been an awful scene that even if I was there I couldn't have understood. Or I would have understood it in some way that was impossible, as if I were underwater or on another planet.

I came to learn that official phrase because my dad would use it when he mislaid something. He'd looked around him as if whatever he was searching for was nearby and he'd say, "Well, I guess that's missing in action." I can see my mom turning the corners of her mouth down when he said that. You could feel she wanted to say, "Don't use those words."

Sometimes, you feel things are bad in more ways than you can count. His words were everyday easy but at the same time uneasy, like a little light coming through a cracked door, but more darkness than light, much more darkness. I sensed he couldn't help it, that it had something to do with his not fighting and his brother dying and the uncertainty about his brother's death, never knowing how he died, just that something happened, which was more like some lame excuse I would give about not doing a chore, how I meant to do it. My father's phrase wasn't something to say about someone dying. Over and over, a sliver of agony—my uncle falling down and not getting up—lurked in the corners of our modest house.

We used to pretend we were soldiers when I was a boy. There were lots and fields around where a bunch of us could divide up and play at killing one another with our BB rifles. I liked it. You don't get to feel powerful when you're a kid, and then you're out with this rifle that was a real rifle in its way, and no adults are bothering you, and you can get pretty worked up about it, even though it's a game. We weren't supposed to shoot the BBs at one another—you could put someone's eye out, the adults said—but we shot at one another anyway. Shooting was way better than just going Bang. We could feel courageous and real. We could be men.

I wondered about my father not going and whether he felt he was a coward. "Yellow," is what the kids I played with would have called him. There are some questions you don't ask. With some guys, their father not fighting might have made them want to join the Marines when enlistment age came around and show everyone, especially their fathers, they weren't afraid, but I didn't feel like that. I felt the world out there was bigger than anyone's rifle. You could disappear whether you had a rifle or not. You could be swallowed up by nothingness the way my uncle had been swallowed. No one would know about you, no matter how brave you had been. When the late afternoon came in the waning time of the year and we had to go home, I could feel that nothingness. The thrill of shooting vanished. I wasn't crossing any battlefield. I was some kid walking down a small town street and wondering what was for dinner.

It was as if my uncle was still around, though, when my father said that about missing in action. It was as if we all were supposed to look for my uncle and not some pair of pliers my father had misplaced. You try to think when you're a kid that if you look for something, you'll find it. It's not like your house is the whole state of Minnesota. It's a limited space. The pliers would "turn up," as my dad liked to say, but my uncle wasn't going to turn up. I could taste the finality of that like the below-zero wind that stung my cheeks and made my eyes water. No getting around it, no ducking and pretending.

"Don't persecute yourself, Max," my mother would say. That was a big word, but I got it, how it must have been easy to go to that lost place and stay there. I vowed I would never do anything like that, but what did I know? How could I miss what I never had? That's part of what my songs have been about— missing what I never had. My father felt that a finger was point- ing at him, but if you never had what's been lost to begin with, then there's no finger in the world that can point at you. Or it's the finger inside of you because you feel all the loss that makes up each day, and it's awful, it's unbearable; and even as a child you sense that in your parents' voices, and it hurts even though they aren't speaking that way to hurt you. They want to shield and protect you, yet the words slip out, or not even words, but those silent times my father would be staring out a window or into space so that he wasn't the efficient business guy he usu- ally was but someone else, someone who if you asked him his name might hesitate—or say his brother's name.

. . .

Looked for a hope inside a war—
Didn't get any place—
A bugle played a slow refrain—
A soldier's name erased.

The town I grew up in was more notable for its roads than its buildings. That was the nature of the place, out there in the Northland of the United States, not much around: some Indian reservations and forests and lakes. Beautiful country, but you have to make your peace with the winters, which I never did. After I left and met people from Canada, guys I played with, they got it, about where I grew up. They got it that even though there were people around you in your house and in town and in school, you could feel very lonesome. Amid the stretches of land and sky, you were pretty piddling: Abraham Whatever-His-Name-Is residing in a two-story wood house with its arithmetical address—225 West 8th Avenue—as if numbers meant something. My ego was eager as anyone's, but I could feel I was never going to be tall enough or far enough. Another person as short as his mind.

The roads were straight. You could stand on one side of town and look down the main highway and see to the end of the other side of town and then off into the receding land. There was no arguing with the roads. With a car, everyone could eat up the distances. Everyone could feel in charge, but the roads had their own lives. In summer, heat mirages beckoned. You thought you were moving through them, but you never got there. In winter there were the snowbanks that turned the roads into tunnels. There was the slickness of the blacktop when it rained, the glistening that was something like beautiful.

The roads taught you about death, how what seemed like every six months or so someone—usually a high school kid—would lose control and crash. The roads made you want to go fast, not out of impatience—nothing of importance was happening—but out of a longing to make something happen, anything. Going fast was a way to fulfill the longing, of being wild in a predictable world, of exploding the map. Yet the longing was more than that. There was the getting into a car and not coming back. You might say you were coming back, but then you didn't. The cheerful "See you later" would echo for decades. Death was somewhere you could drive.

I would walk along the side of the highway and feel the gust of the occasional car and the wind that roamed across the land day and night. Sometimes, when no one was in sight, I'd walk down the center of the road. I liked that. I was part of the road then, and the road seemed as much of a god as anything I knew about. We all honored the road. We all needed the road. The road told us that we made sense, maybe not good sense, but some kind of sense. We were part of a living geometry of right angles, a grid that had nothing to do with the land but everything to do with how the settlers saw the land—something to organize and subdue.

My dad and his brother owned a trucking company, M & M, which stood for Max and Mike. Their trucks hauled cargo around the Upper Midwest. Roads, according to my

dad, were "the nation's life blood." He was serious when he
said that, and I loved it when he was serious about something more than worry and money. He never went very far
away, though, Minneapolis at the farthest. The roads didn't
beckon to him the way they beckoned to me. They weren't a
way out of the lonesomeness. For him the roads connected
places that already were there. For me the roads connected
places that weren't there yet, places that depended on my getting there.

You'd see men hitching a ride sometimes. They could
have been harvest workers. They could have been hobos. They
could have been servicemen on a pass trying to get to their
home farm on some county road off another county road.
They looked forlorn standing by the side of the road. We usually drove by them because our car was full, but I wanted to
stop and hear what they had to say. I wanted to know if they
felt the lonesomeness, how these black stripes on the land
went in every direction and never ended and how that could
make a person who thought about it feel a little crazy, like
every way was a way out but there was no way out. They probably wouldn't have understood me. I don't know who would
have. Things were just what they were: A road was a road, the
prose of American progress.

In my random moments, which I was full of, I could
imagine being a road, lying there and not moving and having
cars and trucks go over me and feeling the friction and heat
but having lots of quiet times too, like at night when you
could see the moonlight reflected on the highway. It wasn't

anything like romantic. It wasn't like you would say to your girl, "Let's go and look at the moonlight on the highway," but it was haunting, and I liked that. People thought they had control—they made the roads—but they didn't. "Well, that highway goes to the west, and you could stop at such-and-such a town. There's a truck stop there." That sort of talk was what I heard when I was growing up, definitions in every direction.

All there is to do here is leave, is what I thought to myself. I wondered if everyone in the United States thought the same thing. That's what the roads were saying—get up and go. If you stayed, it was as if something were wrong with you. You weren't getting what the roads were telling you. You weren't listening. How special some other place might be didn't matter. It was some other place, and that was what counted. I could see myself as a human pinball careering down the roads from Here to There. That was what America was about, the tug between lonesomeness and moving around. If you moved around enough, the lonesomeness wouldn't get to you. You might even start to feel that one place was as good as another, where everyone got an equal vote and an equal cup of coffee at the local diner. I learned that wasn't true, but as a kid I thought that. I'd stand out there by the highway on the east side of town and stare into the distance. I didn't see my future, and I didn't have a past. I saw the road so gradually disappearing.

. . .

He went out looking for a thrill—
Shifting streets, doors delayed—
He never came back, he never called—
His life too much to say.

How did the people speak who lived on the highway-riven land? For me, I'd as soon tell lies as anything, cautionary words coming from an author but—if I may use the word— honest. Lying seems the only way out when you're backed into a corner. You know it's not really a way out, but you may be telling people what they want to hear, so that is a way out. They nod and agree. Or they know you're lying but don't care. Or they're amused. Or they get angry the way my dad would get angry when I made up a lie about how I was supposed to do something or be somewhere but something got in the way. I was telling the truth, though, because day dreams—all that could be—did get in my way.

There were other reasons for lies, like putting people on. I've enjoyed that, lies that came from exasperation with whatever reality was being promoted about who I should be or how the world really was. No, no, no, my lies said. You don't know me. My lies were protests about being trapped in other people's ideas. I was never a politician telling lies to cover my ass. I was a private citizen trying to cover my head.

I learned that if the things you make up become tales and songs, that's good. People like that. My question is: What if everything is a tale? What if you're living in a tale that you make up as you go along? What if there is no truth-ruler that you can measure yourself by? You'll say there are truths, and there are. I was born to Susan Starker, wife of Max Starker, in a hospital in Duluth, Minnesota, but that's only the beginning, and that's not what anyone goes by. People want to know what it was like. That's the basic question. That's what I've been writing and singing about: What was it like?

Lies come from mixed feelings, which is what I've had about mostly everything. You see the black and white of things and how they leak onto each other; how even passion, which can seem like one big wave, is complex. I've never cared for politics because it's about reducing everything to a choice—this or that. Too much gets lost: Reducing is another way of lying, telling people things are simple when they aren't or not being able to be simple, not being able to say atomic bombs are bad news, let's get rid of them. Once you are on one side, you get stuck. You have to see things a certain way. You have to agree with some people and disagree with others. You have to feel you know something definite. You're caught. It may feel good being on the team you're on—the correct team—but you're caught. My way out has been to make things up that aren't going to harm anyone, that are teases, that make you feel you can't be sure—because you can't. It's tricky, though: Your tale, your lie, can run away with you and be what my mom called a "whopper." I must confess—in truth—that I like whoppers. They tell us something that otherwise we would stick in the back of the pantry. They let our feelings cavort. There's got to be more to life than raising your hand and saying "here," as if time were a duty. How are you here?

There's forgetting too, and then being embarrassed that

you forgot and telling lies to cover that up. The nation forgets all sorts of miserable events and then lies about it, and
that's supposed to be okay. It's not even embarrassed, like
about how Negroes have been treated. "Oh, well," the nation
says, "that's how it was. It wasn't so bad. There were plenty of
happy Negroes." Or the nation says that bad things never happened to begin with, or it just shoves those things in a corner
and forgets about them like the Indians getting shoved onto
reservations. I'd sit in school and hear the history teacher talk
about something like "manifest destiny" and wonder what
he was talking about, like America was some kind of blank
blackboard waiting for the white folks to fill things in. If I told
Mr. Rumpelmeyer that he was lying, he would have sent me to
the principal. This was back in the 1950s. I could have been
expelled for being un-American.

Whenever people get nervous, they tell you that you're
un-something. I read that Plato kicked the poets out of his
utopian republic because they were liars—untruthful. Plato
and Socrates cared everything for the truth, so liars got in the
way. Socrates liked to probe people by asking questions and
unraveling their assumptions, which I understand because
I've done some of that myself, but that's no reason to banish the poets. The lies that poets tell are what get us through
the night. Socrates didn't understand the night. He walked
around in the daytime bothering everyone, but he didn't get
the night at all. He never stood outside in January and looked
at the stars and wondered about how his little head understood anything, much less how beautiful and strange it was to
be standing there in the first place.

I can hear you saying that I'm just trying to justify the tales I've told about myself, how I came from Arizona not Minnesota, or that an itinerant blues man gave me my first guitar. I guess I have to say that you weren't in my skin. You didn't see things the way I saw them. You didn't feel the dry desperation I felt in my mouth. You weren't cornered the way I've been cornered. It's not like I started a war when I told some journalist something I invented. It's not that I can't be bothered. I've got a driver's license the same as you. It's that there's something awful in being dutiful, something that deadens a person, something that tries too hard to reassure other people, to make nice. Everything in me has rebelled against that. I probably could have gone to jail many times for my incorrect attitude. The nightly news won't tell you, but many poets are rotting in jails.

. . .

> Someone took my words wrong, didn't
> Get what I tried to mean—
> That surprised then hurt then amused—
> My mind had left the scene.

"You can't stop the future," my father would say, his voice filled with something like marvel, pleased with his thought and pleased with the future-come-true right before him, a new truck with an improved suspension system and turn-on-a-dime steering. Beyond that were skyscrapers, frozen food, interstate highways, color television—all the bright future happening now. He was time's fool, eager to praise whatever came along, a boy at the carnival. I begrudged him.

Part of that was the regular way that sons begrudge their fathers, the sons needing to clear a space for themselves at their fathers' expense. Part was my wariness. We could buy a new car or washing machine, but nothing advertised in *Time* or *Newsweek* or *Life* pertained to me. Everyone in the ads was acting, and then you were supposed to go act like the actors and want what they wanted. My wanting was different. I could feel it inside, but if you don't know what your heart's desire is, then it's hard to get beyond muttering and mumbling.

I sensed how America was a political and social invention. That was no big perception. Most people come to understand that along the strange-but-true way. It bothered me, though, and scared me and thrilled me too, as if the nation were a comic book or the Sunday funnies: Superman, Dagwood, Blondie, Dennis the Menace, Wonder Woman, Li'l Abner running around on the same stage and talking at one another and making no sense whatsoever. Everything seemed like that; Ike and Jimmy Hoffa and Willie Mays and Marilyn Monroe and Bugsy Siegel all mixed up together, everything having something to do with moving along and getting ahead and doing something more, everyone a character, but who was drawing the whole thing was anyone's guess.

What I wanted was the real thing; but what was that, and how was I to find it? I wanted the origins, but the origins of what? Coca-Cola? Rice Krispies? It couldn't be something manufactured. Something that bubbled up from the earth was more like it, something unmistakable, something that didn't know any better and didn't care about knowing better, that wasn't looking over its shoulder or keeping up with the people next door, something that just happened.

Products would be advertised as original because someone had patented them, but what I wanted couldn't be patented. No one else could do it because the person who did it was original, was a whole life that went into a moment's voice. When I started to hear a voice like that—Lead Belly or Odetta or Hank Williams—something changed inside me. They were different from one another, but that was the point. They couldn't be anyone other than who they were. When they sang and played, something welled up inside of them and came out.

Some of these people were popular and some weren't and some were in between. It didn't matter to me. What mattered was that I could test myself against them. They weren't counterfeit. Whatever had gotten into them, I wanted to get into me. The starting point then was, once again, to listen, not to take mental notes—that would come later—but to listen. Our being on the earth here in America had to mean something more than what my dad was excited about. There had to be some sense to all these movable parts, something that said, "This is the undiluted feeling of being alive. You do what you want, but this is it. For here and not for elsewhere. For now and not later." That was what music offered. Nothing compared to music.

I was in band in school for a while and took a few piano lessons, but none of that worked for me: ceremonious and disconnected, limited and abstract, constrained and short on feeling, more an idea about music than the music itself, more something you did because people thought you should. That sounds like the standard sour grapes, not wanting to practice, but that was how I felt; and when I started to hear the origins, when I started to hear what came first, I felt something like redeemed. I felt I'd started to touch bottom. I started to feel I had something to stand on. In ways my situation was ridiculous, because who was some Negro who'd been in prison compared with my cozy life? He'd been violent and he'd suffered and seen things I couldn't imagine. That was the issue, though. Through him I could start to imagine and I could start to hear how a life could take shape that didn't apologize, a life that simply presented itself and the way life occurred, sunny days and dark ones.

There were hellhounds on the trail of some of those lives—lynch law, dice, the bottle—but once I started to understand those hellhounds, I liked the music even more. I didn't know anything about consequences, but why would I? When you hear something that moves you, all you want is to stay there. You want it to drill into you and never leave. When Lead Belly sang, "There ain't no doctor in all the land / Can cure the fever of a convict man," he drilled into me.

I tried to share my discoveries with a few pals in high school, but they weren't interested. I didn't blame them. It was like how my dad would get fired up about something he'd seen advertised and my mom would try to tell him about how she took a walk that afternoon and saw some drops of water hanging from a twig on a tree and how beautiful that was. He'd nod his head as if he'd heard her, even though he hadn't. Those records I started to hear were like those drops of water. They were that real, but they'd been made by people. It was natural that I wanted to be one of those people. You could say I was foolish, but I was a natural fool. That gave me hope.

. . .

An old voice, smoke and grief, searched me out—
Have you seen my lost son?
I went to speak but others answered—
Your boy is everyone.

Neither of my parents had much use for God or religion. They came from different sides of the same street—my dad from Jews somewhere in Lithuania and my mom from German Jews, "European" people as she put it—but they agreed about letting the Big Answer slide. They would say "God damn" or "God forbid," but that was a manner of speaking. They'd also say "godforsaken." There was no synagogue in our town, only the usual string of churches. My sister and I were left to our own spiritual devices.

My parents weren't agnostics or atheists. They just agreed to not care about the Overwhelming Crux, whatever it might be. My father made a show of saying that everyone was entitled to believe what he or she wanted to believe. My mother usually smiled if something religious came up, as if it were a private joke. I sensed they both had been through some kind of mill about God, but neither of them was disposed to discuss the matter. Not many people were disposed back then. You can spend a lifetime trying to pry open your parents' histories and still get nowhere.

We celebrated Christmas with a tree and presents. We'd trim the tree around the second week of December and put gifts under it like regular Christians. "No use feeling left out" was how my mother put it. "We're Jews who have to get along" was my father's take. When I was around eleven I went to church with a friend on Christmas Eve and observed the feeling. I got a certain tingle, but I got a tingle when I went with another friend to some Jewish events. The dignity and the mystery, people raising their voices, the high ceiling—all seemed designed to give you a tingle. Why one tingle was better than another eluded me.

All these easy-going ways should have made things easy on me, but they didn't. America's a religious country. God is on the money. In school we recited a psalm every morning. With our hands over our hearts, we said a pledge every morning in front of the flag that certified that we were "one nation under God." We had a Christmas assembly every year and sang carols. Even if I'd wanted to, I couldn't avoid the certainty of the favored-by-God Christian nation. The feeling I got, though, was that everyone was uncertain, more anxious than peaceful. The holiness didn't add up to an even number. Not only were there so many churches, but within the churches there were sub-churches. When a girl in eighth grade informed me there were dozens of Lutheran denominations, I told her I hoped God had an adding machine. Dozens! And why did the nation have to drag God into every issue? Was He there looking at each election and reading every speech? Should we have been asking God about the senator from South Carolina who believed Negroes should ride in the back of the bus and drink from different water fountains and who made a point of going to church on Sunday?

You can say those are kid questions, maybe smart-alecky, but I've had them forever. And it's worse than that, runs deeper: I've had a bad case of the metaphysical blues. If you're told how things are, then you go along or you let it go; but if you're not told, you're going to look for your own answers, or at least ask your own questions. That was the place I was in: trying to make my uncertain steps somehow certain. The nation-at-large intended to banish that uncertainty, which is what nations do—issue flag-certified, God-blessed certainty. There was no flag of ever-wondering; there was no room for doubting. You stood up for your country and what your country stood for. I stood up every day with the other kids, but I sneaked glances at their faces. "Ever think about?" was how I began a conversation. Or tried to.

I can testify that wonder and doubt are good companions who can keep you alive but can make you seriously edgy. Sometimes I've made a show of being one of the gang, the reassuring "aw shucks" America loves, but the Great Calm has never sat down and talked heavenly matters over with me. I could recognize something larger than myself. I can bow down to Being, to the sunsets and the grasshoppers. I've praised the dust in more than one lyric. What I can't do is pull everything down to a capitalized name or a building or a man in a pulpit. There's too much happening in too many places to do that. There's too much periphery, and I love that outer place, the random this and that, the song source.

Jews and Christians alike have told me I'm a paltry character, never submitting to God and finding my truth in His truth. Still, it's not like I'm the village atheist. I've read the Old Testament and the new one. I can imagine the Hebrew god putting it to those fretful, quarrelsome people, and I can imagine Christ on his pure mission. I've met my share of people on missions. I've been on one myself, but my trembling runs deep, runs to where I was as a kid, which was nowhere and between everything. I couldn't make myself easy. I couldn't doze off in the back of the classroom while the radiator hissed and the teacher droned. I kept feeling that any second something was going to happen. If it didn't happen, I would make it happen. I've gotten into scrapes from thinking that way, from moving from musical style to style and upsetting people. I wouldn't have minded having the steady Prince of Peace in my corner, but when I looked at every day, not just Sunday but all the days, I couldn't see where He was. Some people said He was in their hearts, but that seemed like hiding. Hearts tend to be hidden enough already.

· · ·

Imagined my path on a fearsome night—
A wavering light near me—
I fell but felt no solid ground—
I shouted—the air was empty.

On records, I heard the old voices. Most of the people singing weren't old at all. Most of them were young and full of a reasonable amount of spunk. The records themselves were old, but how old could they be? Thirty, forty years—records hadn't been around that long in the first place. And nothing in America is really old anyway. So "old" to me meant something more like "timeless."

The songs were work songs, courting songs, jail songs, railroad songs, lost-your-woman songs, got-to-get-home songs, need-to-find-a-new-man songs; all songs that came from tasks, predicaments, and situations. The songs were located. They were free in their feeling but precise. They felt necessary. If the people who sang these songs didn't sing them, something inside would seize up.

The quality of the voices grabbed me in both senses of that word—their excellence and their character. They seemed to be more of everything: more real, more plaintive, more unto themselves, sometimes rawer and sometimes sweeter. That had to be an illusion—Elvis at the beginning was plenty real, and he was new. If my feeling was an illusion, though, it felt inarguable. Whatever was in those voices, I wanted to lay my hands on. Whatever was there wasn't around anymore—or at least where I lived. Something was there that came from the cavern of time, made by people who needed music, who needed those songs. TV and movies were entertainment; the songs were spirit errands.

When I started looking into whose voices these were, I learned that most of them had been accomplished performers in their time—the 1920s. They hadn't just fallen out of bed and started singing and getting recorded. That made sense, but they seemed more than their voices. They could be singing about going fishing or losing a lover or catching a train, but there was a feeling of something modest—a voice—taking on something enormous: the restless, free-form American din. What was one voice among so many?

Those voices—Ma Rainey, Bessie Smith, Uncle Dave Macon, Blind Lemon Jefferson, the Carter Family, reverends, jug bands, Creoles, cowboys, union men and women, gospel groups—became another family. Everything was the newest model and latest version in America, so the old, even if it wasn't that old, could be hard to find. The past was more or less worthless, not doing anyone any good, not salable. The past had come and gone, but nothing that has existed can ever leave. Oblivion was a thriving locale. If I was a mystic, I was one with a growing record collection.

The records were scratchy, and the voices sometimes sounded as if they were coming from a long distance—very thin. Things weren't perfect, but that was why the songs existed, because things weren't perfect. People had their circumstances, and there wasn't much they could do about them. Maybe they could run away—many days I thought about running away when I was growing up—but your circumstances followed along. You still were in the same skin. I thought about that too, being in the same skin. You could change your name, but you were in the same skin.

Many of the songs were joyful: musicians having a good time. That captivated me as much as the ballads about ruined women or young men who died in wars. Joy can feel elusive, yet it's inside every instrument. The banjos strumming, the whistles tooting, and the fiddles sawing; that all came from the feeling of release. Music freed people. Whatever oppression existed—and there was no shortage of oppression—music answered.

I needed that freedom because I felt a ceiling on my motions and my feelings, as if I was walking around in a perpetual crouch. I needed to holler and cry, but I didn't know that because I was trying to do as I was told and keep my feelings to myself, the way a boy who was going to be a man was supposed to. Until my mother died, I never saw my father cry. I understood that. You worked your way through life. You went to your job and you came home, and your life was not about letting go but about holding on. You complained or you didn't, but the situation remained.

The voices on the records, even the people who had in all likelihood been through their share of hell—sometimes definitely, because that's what they were singing about—were tuned to joy. I don't mean childish or childlike. I mean the voices enjoyed having the feelings—good and bad, up and down—they had. They owned those feelings for as long as they sang them. That wasn't long—a couple minutes, but those minutes were special and clear as springwater. Those minutes sliced through every habit. Memorialized on the records, they were as permanent as anything that could be cast aside could be permanent.

I was around twelve when I first heard those voices, but right off I wanted to join them. I didn't tell anyone because I would have sounded crazy. Here I was living in atomic-age America, not some hollow in the South or across-the-tracks roadhouse where time stood still because time had nothing better to do. That was the point, though. My feeling wasn't nostalgia or thinking those people had life better. What I wanted was to make time stand still the way those voices had. Hearing them, hearing Bessie Smith sing "I had a dream last night / That I was dead / Evil spirits / All around my bed," I knew a person could do it. Somehow, I could be that person.

. . .

Sit and sing into that microphone—
Let it come as it pleases—
Like you were courting and drinking wine—
Like your hard life was easy.

I grew up in mining country, iron ore country. People came
from all over the world to work in the mines. What they had
to do was simple: Take one thing from the earth—iron ore—so
another thing could be made—steel. If you look at the pictures
of the miners, pictures from early in the twentieth century,
the men have that old-time stature. It's not just their mus-
taches and beards and their dark, proper clothes. There's that
feeling of having an occupation that has asked something of
them and that they have answered. Maybe that's idealism on
my part. Plenty of them probably drank themselves to death.
Plenty left to do something else, that American restlessness,
but plenty stayed and didn't drink themselves to death. They
stayed in the town I grew up in and built houses and raised
families and tried to love their children and wives. No one
fully succeeds in that department, especially at the end of a
long, weary day, but some stayed and tried. I could feel that
when I was growing up, how some stayed and tried. What was
that resident life to me?

The miners' work was dirty, hard, and dangerous. I wanted
to ask the fathers and grandfathers of some of the kids I grew
up with about their work, but I was shy and embarrassed.
Asking a grown-up about his life seemed too forbidding.
Probably it was—asking anyone to look at his or her life can be

forbidding—but there was more holding me back than that. There was the wound out there in the land: the huge, orderly gouges in the earth that the mines had made.

When we studied geology in school, we learned it took billions of years to make what we were taking out of the earth. You sat there and your teacher, who actually wore a bow tie every day, said "billions of years" and you were thinking about a cute girl or how you'd rather be anywhere else, so the words seemed to slide off. But they didn't slide off for me. That's a powerful long time, what they call "eons." My grandma, who could be irreverent, would have said that was before God was born. And here we were with these mines that some men owned and other men worked in. Here we were watching the railroad cars pass by bound for Duluth and loaded with ore, clinking and clanking through the night, sending out a rumble you could feel miles away. Here we were.

I didn't know what to make of that, how to put the pieces together. Later, when I met some Indians from west of where I grew up, I learned they were spending their lives putting those pieces together, remembering the earth. They didn't make any mines. They were what my dad would have called "backward." "What about the near-infinity of time and the planet?" I might have asked him. "What about it, Abe?" he would have answered. "Those mines are jobs." End of discussion, end of me, end of the Indians.

We were raised to be proud of the mines. They were a feat. You couldn't argue that, but the terrible things that people did, like wars and bombs, were feats too. The mine being a feat seemed to beg the question. In that way, I was lucky that I lived in town in a house next to other houses. I was a town kid who could look away from the endless taking from the earth and pretend with everyone else that people knew what they were doing. I wasn't very good at pretending out loud—my mom could see through me in a minute—but I liked the pretending I could do in my head that put me in another place, like the James Dean poster in my bedroom, the one of him walking through Times Square, far away from the mines of Minnesota. He's wearing an overcoat and smoking a cigarette. It's a crappy, messy day, the hubbub of New York all around him. Even though it's a photo, you can hear the noise. In the background you can see a marquee for the movie *20,000 Leagues Under the Sea*. I saw that movie—stupid, the usual much ado about nothing. James Dean, though, he was something. I could see myself walking beside him, posing and not posing at the same time, spooked but trying to be sure of myself.

I didn't want to be an actor. James Dean came from a small city in Indiana. He knew, the way I did, there were bigger cities, ones where a person could toss one's self into the bottomless river of the human race. There was a sad feeling in that photo, something raw, but there was something comforting too, how he could be himself and no one was calling him out or even caring. He didn't have to take anything more on himself than just being himself. That was a task already, more weight than the pounds of him, but as real as mining the ore.

You pick the people you need to help you when you are growing up. You don't necessarily meet them. James Dean was out of this world before I ever would have had a chance to see him in the flesh. What matters is that you feel you have some company. Were those gouges in the earth my company? They were, but I didn't know what to do with them. I didn't know where to turn with them. Like mining, so much that was daily could be brutal. I sensed that about James Dean—not that he was brutal, but that whatever went into him being that keyed up and wary and yet outgoing and alive had something brutal in it, something that didn't care about who you were or what you thought, something that spoke for the indifferent strength of the earth, a great dumb beast. I read where Dean was something called a "method actor," someone who had to know everything about what his character would say or do in a situation. I was in a situation on the earth that seemed so big there was nothing I could say. Hold a piece of that ore in your hand sometime, and feel it.

. . .

When the run-down clock comes for you,
Son, you'd better be ready—
The sun won't wait, the boss won't stop—
Your faith can't be too steady.

Small towns are filled with characters, the human comedy that has been around forever. I wanted to be a character myself. Some people say I am, but I don't know how my type would be defined: recluse who appears on stages, poet who is not what the college crowd calls a poet, regular cryptic guy. Not that it matters; you do what you do.

In our town there were, among others, the Philosopher, the Minister, the Drunkard, the Card Cheat, the Loose Woman, the Braggart. Each one was a distinct person—the Minister, for instance, had a limp as if maybe God had struck him at some point—but they were also categorical. The person's name got folded up and tucked inside. Each one of them could have walked out from the pages of a tale. Each one had a moral to impart. None of them was interested in changing—more the opposite. Their ways may have taken them down, the way it happened with the Drunkard, but the ways were their ways. Pride cuts in different directions.

Where you grow up—Somethingsville, Minnesota—is your universe. You're trying to figure where your place is in it and what the planets are. I heard about these people from my parents and from other kids. I'd see them on the streets. Later, when I was in high school, I'd meet some of them in the local pool hall where they used to hang out. There were pool halls in most towns back then. There was time for people to seemingly do nothing.

People said the Philosopher came from a rich family and didn't have to work. I'd see him in the library hunched over a book, his lips moving with the words. Whenever he looked up, he seemed startled. How could he hold all his thoughts? The Minister didn't have a congregation but carried the Bible around. You'd see him stop someone on the street, open the Bible, and start spouting, animated-like. He'd stop my mother; somehow she seemed more amenable as a Jew than my father. He was polite to everyone. "Nice day, Mrs. Starker," he'd say. Rain or snow, the weather didn't matter; that's what he would say. He didn't live in the world the way other people lived in the world. He had a role in a larger play—the story of feeling and retribution. When I was a tyke looking up at him, I could see a small blaze in his clear blue eyes.

The others I mentioned hung especially around the pool hall. For a time, I must have been fifteen, I spent many afternoons there. I didn't care for pool, because I didn't like being watched and I didn't like competing. I did like the atmosphere. Time hung in the air like dust. The place smelled of old sweat, whiskey, and tobacco. It was a man's place, but the Loose Woman seemed at home. She never shot a game, but she'd sit on a chair and hold court. Her name was Rae, and she and the men would joke with one another. She wasn't old, but she wasn't young.

She'd tease me about what I'd been up to, which hadn't been much, though I puffed myself up as best I could. She liked to banter. I was torn up, because the word was she would go to bed with a guy in high school—a real woman, not a girl, who would go to bed with a high school guy! That was a dream coming true. She'd smile at me while I stammered and blushed. I could feel the men in the hall winking at her. I wanted her bad. I felt, though, a melancholy about her. She wasn't a regular mom, a housewife, or a teacher or secretary. Her life was in some other place where women weren't supposed to be, but there she was. I felt sorry for her. That was silly, because who was I to feel sorry for a grown woman leading her own life? Why was I sensitive to something that probably wasn't there? Why couldn't I be like other guys and tease her back and touch her and make the right insinuations? Why couldn't I turn my head and wink at the other men?

It's tempting to put more onto people—the sums of their broken obligations—than deserves to be put on. I've been doing that my whole life. That's one place the songs come from, my putting on more. It comes from a craving in me for more feeling than the workaday world allows but that songs do allow. In songs you can wallow and aggravate at the same time, and that was the pool hall—an idle yet tenacious song.

I never spoke a word to some of these characters, but they were precious figures in the world of my head. They were my fellows. They hailed from somewhere else than the regular people who had regular jobs. They might have been forlorn or not, but they had that jolt of complicity that woke me from my half-formed dreams. "Hopeless" my dad would say about someone like the Card Cheat, well known as a practical joker and often-arrested thief. Maybe he was hopeless, but that seemed a badge of some kind of honor. To be hopeless meant you had fallen and you didn't care about getting up. All the ongoing talk was just talk—stuff people read in the newspaper or heard on the radio or watched on TV and made a passing fuss about, news that didn't concern you. I liked that, being unto yourself, never improving, not caring what other people thought. I didn't understand the pain in them, but pain was not the total of them. You better watch out what you pity. Any of those people could have told me a thing or two. Living each stubborn day, they did.

. . .

The Drunkard had words with the Minister—
The Minister bowed his head—
Life never played right for me—
Don't pray, the Minister said.

Though people make a to-do about categories, no two song paths—the pizzazz of Tin Pan Alley or freshet of Appalachia—are very far apart. Some metaphorical linkage is ever lurking. Love may be snappy or sappy, calculating or innocent, abandoned or found, but what happens remains part of any you've-got-your-feelings life. Hearts break the same in a hollow in West Virginia or on 52nd Street. The hands of song reach out in longing or regret. My steady fingers on the guitar strings search the unsteadiness inside me. One coming-and-going day buries another and we—who anyway are scraps and slivers of songs ourselves, Black Jack Davey and Maid of Constant Sorrow—are mostly good with it. What choice do we have?

Metaphor, one thing turning into another, both startles and reassures. Through its far-and-near reaching, you feel how everything is connected and how that's not presumptuous bull but more like literal, more how we tend to be busy and aren't listening, more like how what seems incongruous isn't. If we were listening, we'd hear some—always a fraction, though—of what's spoken by the trees and rivers and the creatures too, the famous birds and bees. When I learned that whales sing to each other, I wasn't surprised.

If I sound like a nature boy for someone who grew up in town and has spent most of his life entering and exiting hotel rooms, that's okay. Lying in a late summer field or walking down a dirt road or looking up at the stars—no one else around, only me—has been the reassurance that lies beneath the words. Nature wasn't calling me to write. Nature's been doing okay without me, and "nature" is a word, after all. The planet is called "Earth" not "nature." What happened was that I could feel everything coming into me and how that helped put me in perspective: one of the throng, the blades of grass and grains of sand. My equipment was everyone's. I too was rooted in the natural changes and earth-struck—hot and cold, in and out, light and dark, living with the differences and the equals. I belonged here, which is something for someone who's never felt part of a group or cause.

If you can find a way to link one thing with another and it makes sense to you—feeling-sense not head-sense—then it's good. At times the leap of metaphor may seem far-fetched, which is what some people have said about lines in my songs. "How the hell did he dream that up?" Sometimes I was joking, but my joking was serious. Misery, also known as the blues, had a thousand faces I could never name. What mattered was making the feeling real by putting a word-face on it: a witch, a gambler, a shepherd boy, a priest.

We find similarities to guide us, maps of plausible locations. Growing up, I needed that guidance. School meant nothing. I liked reading books—Steinbeck, Mark Twain—but once we started to discuss them, once everyone started raising hands and giving answers, I lost interest. We were trying to put lightning in a bottle. I wanted to live so the lightning would flash around me constantly. There would be no talking, just a startling silence. I couldn't have said that at the time. I can barely say it now.

There's something flashing and beckoning in metaphors, in making one thing into another, the basic, intuitive magic. When Robert Johnson sang that the "blue light was my blues and the red light was my mind, all my love's in vain," that was magic. It gave me chills when I first heard him, and still does. He was leaning his way into a huge feeling—anyone who's lost a lover can understand—but he was also finding his way through what was there in front of him, the two disappearing lights on the train. You can see him standing there. You can see the train leaving. He's not making anything up, but those colors are more than colors.

To write like that you have to stand with the roots of life. You have to be right there, trying to keep your falling-apart head in one piece, your toes digging into the ground, not distracted by what you or someone else thinks you should be saying or feeling. Loss may be the deepest feeling, and Robert Johnson knew that. Love runs around and makes noises, but loss sits there on the splintery bench and broods.

Critics write about influences and what I've taken from this song or that song. I've taken plenty. That's the nature of the task—one big stream of music—but in another way I haven't taken a thing. It's more that I've been open to how nothing stays still, how each moment everything is increasing and decreasing even if you can't see it, like the shores of the seas, and how those changes have spoken to me. I used to sit out on a windy October day when I was a boy and watch the leaves fall. My dad would have me rake them, but first I wanted to see them fall. It seemed only fair. I loved watching their fluttering and flitting. Every leaf's flight was different—a show for me. My dad would come by and remind me to "rake not dream." A little sad to make beauty a chore: The raking got done, but I took my time.

I remember first hearing Nat King Cole sing "Autumn Leaves." My mom owned the record. He was the best—his voice warm and full and silken. He sang in French too, which made sense because the feeling—missing someone—was in all languages. And the feeling wasn't speaking. The feeling was singing.

* * *

Her love became a taunting fire—
The fire turned cold and gray—
The dark became the morning sky—
Blessing another day.

Something called "folk music," a form of guitar strumming accompanied by tuneful keening, marked my youthful years. As music went, it wasn't very advanced, but that was never the point. The structures were simple because the gists were simple. They were simple because they were real: storms at sea, the coming of spring, fast horses, and unrequited love. Folk took whatever was at hand and sang about it. You might ask, however, about the other part of the phrase: Who were these "folk"? It seemed a fair question, since the Germans had made a fuss over the word that could make a person queasy. Though no one could exactly pin the word down, I heard the same answer in different guises: regular people, the common people, working people, what used to be called the "unwashed masses." Since their origins were communal, it made sense that folk songs arose from the well of time. The old songs from the British Isles didn't have ascribed authors, nor did some of the American songs. The old songs just existed, the chaff of centuries. People who were interested in such things felt there was something almost holy there, what had been passed on from generation to generation. I felt that way too at times. Everything was about today in the United States. The songs were rooted in the mystique of yesterdays.

What happened in the songs was something like eternal. People betrayed one another. People ran off and were never heard from again. People fell in love with the wrong person. The whole tissue of cross-purpose and misapprehension reverberated, sometimes madly. The consequences could be dire: bodies that jumped down wells or perished in battles or drowned at sea. Life didn't have many margins. If you fell out of step, you were going to pay.

That dire sense of events spoke to something dire in me. I didn't crave bad news, but I craved news that wasn't cooked up to sell a product. In America, losing track of your feelings came easy. Endless distractions and dodges beckoned. You said you were happy because all other answers were unacceptable. Your face could ache from smiling. Every folk song that had lasted showed a map of true feeling.

When you played for people, you honored history, usually

giving a little preamble about the song's origins and where you picked the song up. Folk singers were like curators. They listened to old records and old people who knew the tunes, and they pawed through books of ballads. They could get very prickly about what version of a song was the most genuine. Being a folk singer wasn't about innovation. The songs had paid dues, and you did too.

I liked that longtime sense of folk music. The historical scrap you found yourself in—this or that era—gained some echoes. The human situations in the songs—birth and death, love and grief—never changed. I could have lived hundreds of years ago, and when I sang "Lord Randall" with its "Oh, I met with my true love," I was living hundreds of years ago. Even the dark songs—and more of them were dark than not—spoke to a spark that couldn't be extinguished.

Being a folk singer could be confining. You were more a conduit than an original artist. The visions were already there. Musical technique mattered, but you weren't playing Chopin. That wasn't to say there weren't people, such as Woody Guthrie, who wrote new folk songs. Woody, though, was one of the people. He'd been hard-traveling and hardworking, or so he claimed. He was from Oklahoma, a real American place. He seemed to have risen up from the great American belly of miscellaneous and sometimes political feeling. I was from the heartland too, but I came later. I was Jewish, I hungered for poetry, I heard rock 'n' roll—a lot of differences.

Once upon a time I played and sang "Wabash Cannonball" and "Michael, Row the Boat Ashore" and "Delia," but being a folk singer felt weirdly tense. I was supposed to toe a certain line, wear a certain collar. Mostly, I respected that. What got passed on was precious, but it was confusing too. Who determined authenticity? Though some people tried, there wasn't a pope of folk music. Folk music spoke with certainty to our American uncertainty about who we were. We were this and we were that—ballads and cowboy songs, country blues and work songs, songs about the warden and songs about the inmates, songs about riding a freight and songs about sitting on the front porch. The people who had sung the songs didn't know the other people who sang different songs in different places. People in recent times gathered the songs and called the miscellany "folk music." Could there be such a thing as a made-up tradition? Why not? You had to start somewhere.

With their stirring and poignant refrains, those songs made me feel at home, even if I didn't know where "home" was. The songs said that my voice belonged with other voices, an offer I was glad to accept, but I knew—and not deep down but right at the surface—that I was no one from nowhere, more a hole than a whole. When I announced myself as a pure product of the American folk, someone who'd grown up rough and tumble here and there, that was sleight of hand. Steeped in possibility, Americans always were creating themselves. I was joining that show. AUTHENTICITY STEP RIGHT UP—and I did.

I wasn't the only one who adopted a story about being one of the mythical folk. Every four years, politicians fell all over themselves showing the folk that they were folk too. If I was someone else from elsewhere, it didn't matter. I needed to prop myself up with something that felt rooted. Someone back home could look at me and say, "He's not who he's saying he is. He's a fake, another so-called folksinger." They weren't in my predicament, though. They were part of something. They stayed where they were. I had to move on, even if I had little idea where I was heading. What faith I had lay in the songs' sustaining power. That seemed an essential American lesson—to make what, by birth, wasn't you into part of you.

．．．

I sang the song about new love—
I sang the one of grief—
I stood and watched you go your way—
My voice beyond belief.

My favorite time is sunrise, being with the sky drama, witnessing the enormity. For some minutes, my head quiets down. I'm on the same planet as everyone else. And, for all the taking-it-for-granted assurance of another day another dollar, that sunrise didn't have to happen. If we say that there are laws of motion and spheres and space and how long the sun has been the sun, that doesn't take away the spectacle of anything being here in the first place. There's nothing preachy about saying that creation is daily.

For some years when I was a boy, I delivered newspapers each weekday morning. I got out of bed when the world was still dark, feeling very grown-up, and walked the blocks to where the papers were waiting for me to stow them in my canvas bag. I made some money—another dollar—but that wasn't why I pushed in the alarm clock button and put my feet down on the usually cold floor. There were feelings there that were mine alone.

I walked those quiet streets alone. I could feel myself then, not anything dicey like who I was—which meant who I wanted to be, the yearning I'm writing about—but simpler, purposefully striding, alert, left to my own devices. Maybe a light would already be on in a second-floor window—someone getting up. Maybe a dog who'd spent the night on a porch would bark. A car might go by. Somebody might wave. Nothing out of the ordinary, but it didn't have to be. I was out of my house, a place that pressed in on me the way your childhood house presses in on you. There's that sense of do that and do this that comes with growing up in a house. I wasn't resentful—my parents were loving people who gave me the strength to do what I've done—but my life seemed like the lined paper they gave us in school to write on. I didn't want to be lined.

Sometimes I whistled or hummed to myself—the pleasure of my sounds in the silence. I had to get to Blinky Moran's house, where the folded papers awaited me, but usually I had a minute to stop and admire the sky's majesty, the fading stars. I taught myself the stars' names from a book in the local library. I could stand there and take in the peace that was laid out above me, everything larger than I could imagine. Did I tell myself—because I talked endlessly to myself in my head—that maybe someday I would imagine? Nothing in the world of my self-addresses was that clear. My nose was at my grindstone, the word-tangle inside me part of my feeling-tangle. Anyhow and every way, the sky and silence were speaking.

Picking up the papers, I glanced at the headlines. I knew

the newspaper mattered, the center of many grown-ups' heads, but the news bleated the same day-in, day-out tune. Eisenhower was president, the Soviet Union our enemy. Somewhere a hurricane or earthquake devastated villages. Buildings collapsed; in the photo on the front page people stared, their faces blank with suffering. Some jowly senator made a speech about what a great nation we lived in. In the local news, our town councilors were looking into something—sidewalks, a park, hiring a new police chief. To me this all seemed a little muddled, how what got into the paper was called "news" when it was so predictable. The news was like my parents talking at the dinner table about this one down the street and that one up the street, only the front page's talk was about nations, money, and famous people. Nothing got decided, but that wasn't the point. Perturbed yet imperturbable, the news went on.

I'd shoulder my bag and cover the blocks that were my territory, chucking the papers onto porches and front steps. Sometimes someone would be out there waiting for me. He'd wave, though sometimes it might be a woman with a coat thrown over a housedress, a scarf over her hair. In winters I'd be trudging through the snow and cold. I felt like a man then.

Walking along, I made up stories about myself. I could stand outside of myself—the good side of being self-conscious. Not that my stories made me a better person; more like I had to do that making-up in order to live. If I didn't have myself to talk to, whom would I talk to? I liked the story of being a paperboy and having people depend on me—"There's Abe, bright and early"—but I wouldn't have minded a story that turned my routine into something out of the ordinary. I'd rescue a cat caught up in a tree. I'd see a house on fire and call the fire department. I'd lead a lost child home. I performed good deeds in my head. I'll give myself that.

Later on, I'd see the sunrise from a different point of view—staying up all night, sometimes walking the streets, sometimes hanging out, sometimes being by myself in my apartment. This was downtown in New York City. Anyone who's lived in a big city like New York knows how precious quiet is, how being by yourself can feel eerie and exhilarating at the same time, being alone on a huge stage set that was real. I didn't have a satchel of newspapers, but I did have the gravity of my footsteps. I wasn't headed anywhere special, just out walking with my thoughts, letting the calm seep into me, letting time become empty.

I might go by a bakery that was open, since the bakers showed up at three or four in the morning, or a hospital where someone was always coming in or going out or a newspaper stand, where I'd look at a headline—MORE TROUBLE. I'd keep walking, and then I'd start to feel the sun coming up among the buildings, casting ribbons of light and dark on the streets and walls. I'd feel a lightening inside me. I might have been tired, but I felt more awake than ever.

Sometimes I rambled with a girlfriend. We'd stop by a cafe that opened early and have a coffee. We'd sit there and watch the day come forth. The streets would start to pulsate with people, buses, and cars. If the surrounding buildings weren't too tall, an angle of light would pierce the cafe's storefront window. Some of the people coming in would be sluggish, waking

up still, but some were raring to go, lively with quips and banter—"Whadya know?" and "Howz it goin'?" and "Geez them
Yankees"—talking New York talk. We'd sit there, a little dizzy
from caffeine and having been up all night but contented. The
blood in our veins was rich. We made our own news.

. . .

Looking up at the vanished night
Boy by the curb of the street—
Thinking his thoughts for no one else—
Happy with unease.

If you would have asked me the word to describe my childhood in America, I'd have said, "bomb." I could have further defined it as the A-bomb or the H-bomb, but the exact
species didn't matter. There was this force that could ruin
everything, that was more powerful than any weapon human-
kind previously had devised, that made a mushroom cloud
that rose into the atmosphere, that left anyone who was tar-
geted either dead or maimed or sick with radiation, that was a
nightmare come true. It had been used by my country whose
flag I saluted every morning, a country "under God." My dad
said many more of our guys would have been killed by the
"Japs," if we hadn't used it. He said that casually—another fact.

We had air raid drills. A siren in town went off, and we huddled under our desks with our heads down. Our teacher paced
around the room to see if we were ducking down correctly.
Signs designated our school as a fallout shelter. Someone told
me that one of the mine owners who lived in town had his

own fallout shelter. I would have liked to have seen it, creepy but probably comfortable, everything good until whenever the "all-clear" sounded. If it did sound.

I remember crouching while waiting for the event to happen, for the earth to shake or the sky to split open or the big brick building I was in to start crumbling, as if a giant had come along and given it a shove. I wondered if the Japanese children had known how to get under their desks. I wondered if some of them had opened their eyes at the sound. I wondered if that had made them blind. One girl in our class used to whimper. We made fun of her, but she said she couldn't help it. "It's going to be awful," she said, "more awful than you can imagine."

After a time we got up and went back to doing our schoolwork, as if nothing had happened, because nothing had happened. We were still there. The school and town were still securely there. Our teacher stood at the blackboard and started explaining about long division. Every day she was filling us up with knowledge. Maybe we fidgeted; maybe we paid attention. Maybe we hadn't forgotten being on the floor, more like a dog than a person. Maybe all those things were going on inside us at the same time.

I remember holding my pencil and being ready to do my arithmetic and thinking that I would not be here and the pencil would not be here and the paper would not be here. You were going along in your day and thinking about what team you might be on when sides got chosen on the playground at lunchtime or whether your mother was going to make the chocolate cake she said she might make, and then you were under your desk waiting for the world to end. How did one thing go with another?

We never talked about it much. When you're a kid, you do as you're told, especially with something that's official. We knew our nation had enemies and they might attack us at any moment. We had to be "vigilant," to quote our teachers. At the same time as we were being vigilant, we used to watch film strips like "Our Friend the Atom," about how there was a time coming when we wouldn't have to pay for electricity because atomic energy would be free. We were lucky. The atom in the film strip had legs and arms and danced around. There might have been a little song he sang. The atom was a guy; I remember that. He had a name like Al the Atom.

"You can't make this shit up" is what you say when you're older, but that doesn't do the absurdity justice. I'm not sure what can. I can remember my face almost on the floor and smelling the wax they used to polish the floors—a thick, almost sweet smell. I remember at first my position was uncomfortable, but then I'd get used to it. I tried to make myself as compact as I could. I think I wanted to be invisible. Who wouldn't? I remember being stiff when I got up and how we were supposed to stretch before we went back to our desks. We goofed around when we stretched, doing exaggerated poses. Anything for a nuclear laugh.

The words weren't there for me in the third grade, but the feelings were. I try not to forget that. The songs reclaim some of the feelings. There's this low-grade hysteria going on, and you're ten years old and trying to act as though everything is okay. It's not as if anyone was asking you what your feelings were. The idea of anyone asking anything was almost hilarious. Eventually you could go out and run around on the playground and let off whatever steam had accumulated. Eventually you went to sleep and had nightmares about bombs. They'd been used, and they could be used again. There had been children in Japan who were my age who didn't get to their next birthday party. The nightmare happened. They became ashes.

I'd lie in my bed and wait. It wasn't as though it had to happen during school hours on a weekday. None of our teachers talked about that. They acted as though the Russians would call us up and tell us the bombs were coming after spelling and before geography. That seemed almost funny. Meanwhile I stared at the ceiling and waited. As my Uncle Simon—one of my mom's three brothers—used to say, "Don't kid yourself, kid."

. . .

I felt the heat, a blast on my face—
My body began to fade—
Everything fell—The sky fell too—
All the making unmade.

I first heard the blues on records. There weren't any blues men and blues women in the town I grew up in. There were practically no Negroes in the town to begin with: two families. I knew one of the kids from one of the families. He told me the two families didn't get along. One mother had said something to the other mother. I told him the Jewish families didn't get along either.

The record could have been by any number of people whose names at first meant nothing to me. Who exactly was someone named "Son House"? Who was "Charley Patton"? I heard music on the radio—country and western, pop, rock 'n' roll, R&B, which was jazzy and hot on the backbeat—but I didn't hear any voices that came from where those voices came from. I had to meet record collectors, who were a sort of underground railroad of the blues. If you were keen on the old stuff, the origins, the real down-Southness, you were into the blues.

When I started listening to those recordings that I begged, stole, and borrowed, a whole avenue of being alive opened up. That sounds huge, but what I heard was huge. I didn't know you could make your sadness sing. Pop music was upbeat, and though the blues was often playful, it was still the blues—the bottom color. The blues spoke to what had gone down with Negroes as a people and what went down between men and women. The blues flew in the face of the optimism and progress touted every day in white America. Progress about what and for whom, might have been a couple questions that didn't get asked. The blues spoke to the basic wisdom—trouble is bigger than you are.

If a good deal of life is taken away from you, you're liable to look closely at what's still there. You're liable to root yourself because you don't have much choice in the matter. No one is asking your precious opinion. The color of your skin has answered everything. Romance and sex and the earth and all the good things that come from the earth are, however, still there. All the things—good and bad—that people do to one another are still there too. All the ways a person can be to him or herself—dignified or undignified, satisfied or unsatisfied—are still there. Many of the eager purposes—where you are going next and what you are going to do—may be banished. That lack of freedom can kill you or make you stronger. Sometimes, it can do both, which creates something like tragedy: "I didn't know I loved her/ 'Til they laid her down."

I knew some big things were wrong, not just the bomb or what was in the papers about Negroes being denied this and refused that. America was a happiness conspiracy, but not everyone was given an invitation. And all that smiling in the ads and on the television seemed like an awfully big effort, a weight, like you never stubbed your toe or fell down and tore your pants. To admit the blues was to admit the missteps woven into life, the times where things didn't work out and weren't going to work out. You could try, but your trying didn't matter. Your girlfriend left, you flunked a test, you meant to say something but didn't. You said the wrong thing.

The songs were honest about anguish, and no one I knew was honest in that way. Feeling down was always something "to get over," like you were running hurdles. Those old black men were my teachers, telling how sometimes a person couldn't keep from crying. How you could hold a photo of someone and wish it would talk to you. How you could sit and play your music to the night, just you and the stars, and how that lonesomeness was real: a day closer to your death. How there were no bodies without shadows, and those shadows were the blues.

I intuited something unofficial, something off the radar, something buried beneath the word "race," and I wasn't going to stand around and wait for the headlines to catch up with me. When I picked up a guitar and started to learn "Death Letter Blues" by Son House, I was entering an unknown land where you could say I had no business. But the good and frightening thing about America is that everything is everyone's business. And I was—to give myself credit—many steps ahead of those who didn't know the blues existed, for whom at most the music was a rumor about some poor blacks down South: disregarded music from disregarded people. That meant millions of people were walking around in their busyness who didn't know the blue notes. Where did that put them when the night fell on their hopes?

There could be an end-of-the-line harshness in the blues— what came from evictions, lynchings, hatred, and contempt as long as a country's history—but there was plenty of whoopee too. Everybody wants to rise, and singing went with that rising. The truth lay in the contrasts, like a record having two sides. You couldn't know what lightened you if you didn't know what darkened you. You didn't have to choose the dark. One way or another—personal history or national history or world history—the dark was going to find you. And when you did lighten, it felt good.

I must have said something ultra-eloquent like, "Wow!" to whatever collector—Doug Gallagher or Lew Ramsdell or Wiley Seeforth, all blues fiends I met along the way—I was first listening with. I'm sure whichever one nodded and laughed a quiet laugh. How had I lived without knowing this music existed? Back then, I didn't understand how urgency was not high up on many emotional shopping lists. Maybe people already felt enough urgency bubbling around inside them—rent to pay and promises to keep. Even if they somehow heard such music, it was too unadulterated, what the fearful call "primitive." Maybe, along those lines, the category in the record world—"race music"—automatically closed the door. Or maybe the music seemed to come from a part of the world and a time that was best left behind. I've met black people who felt the blues was the song of servitude, testifying to hell or trying to forget but always caught. I had no reply to that. More irony was at work in America than I ever was going to uncover, unwanted history left out of doors to decompose. I kept my head down and played what I loved: Charley Patton singing "Lord, your drought come an' caught us / an' parched up all the tree." Does anyone need to apologize when feeling touches down? Is there ever enough to go round?

. . .

Someone asked the black dog
How you like your blues?
Black dog squirmed then smiled—
White, if you only knew.

My mother was unhappy. You wouldn't have said unhappy or happy applied to my dad. Those words weren't for men. That absence wasn't his fault. That's how being a man went—bearing up so feelings were irrelevant. "Some things are best left unsaid," my dad would counsel the rest of us at the dinner table when some emotional jack was about to jump out of the box. Being a man was like the fitted, army-type jacket my dad wore to work with the company's name embroidered on the front. You shrugged or you didn't, but you wore the jacket.

My mom didn't sit on a sofa and cry. She bustled: household chores, preparing meals, dealing with my sister and me and her mother-in-law, and volunteering at the local hospital. She took magazines and books to patients and sat and read to them and talked with them. At her funeral, people showed up that I didn't know who had wonderful things to say about her. I started crying all over again.

Her blues were in the corners of her life. Sometimes she would be at the table with us eating dinner, but she wasn't there. Sometimes I'd see her staring out a window. It didn't feel like the daydreaming I did in school. It felt that she was caught somehow or adrift—or both at the same time. Our house was filled with heavy furniture—bureaus, cupboards, and an oak dining room table with thick curved legs—but my mother seemed like a spirit, especially when she smiled to herself, a little downturned smile. If someone came along, she made the smile broaden. She tossed her head and stood a bit taller. She knew America was in the be-cheerful business. She didn't want to be caught out. The blues people I listened to were among the categorically lost. My mom was among the found, but she was lost too.

She'd say things to me, about how something was "funny." It didn't mean ha-ha. It meant something that seemed to make sense might not make sense. It could be something she read in the paper, like some Southern senator proclaiming that the Negroes were contented. "Funny," my mother would say.

"How would he know?" It could be something in our neighborhood. "Mrs. Bulka was telling me she wouldn't trade her life for anyone's. It's funny then how she turns around and complains." "Maybe that's human nature," my mother would say, her voice speculative but resigned.

I thought a lot of things were funny that way too. I still do. My songs are about the discrepancies, what tilts one way but says it's the opposite. My mom posed a question that's never gone away: If you thought twice, were you bound to be sad? I was a kid who carried the usual dumb, the-world-is-all-about-me confidence. I was selfish, and part of me just wanted her to fly right—less for me to pay attention to. But underneath my impatience, there was the feeling she was teaching me something only a woman could teach me, her feeling for what was "funny."

She loved clothes and "nice things." She looked religiously at ads in the fashion magazines she took and pointed out to my sister or me what she admired. I don't think she was covetous. She wasn't like that. She liked beauty, and there wasn't much of that in a mining town in northern Minnesota. Her plight was bigger than that, though. I had the feeling of how she had to live in a world that men made. She didn't care about the things men did: their betting pools and occupations, their political wrangling and the off-color jokes they told with winks, their Schlitz beer and smoky poker games—all the assumed self-importance that went with a man's world. She had to act as though she did care, but that only made her sadder. "I don't see what you see in that," she'd say to my dad. I don't remember him replying.

She chose to be with my father—there was a framed wedding day picture on the wall in our living room—and have a family with him, but again her situation seemed bigger than that. We fall into the web of time; though, if you're a woman, you fall into something that isn't about you but that you have to live with and more or less honor. My mom would see my father and me watching some ballgame and would pause near the TV and shake her head. If we tried to explain something to her about what was happening, she only shook her head more. "That isn't for me," she'd say. It could have been but she was right—it wasn't for her. I had friends whose moms followed baseball, but not my mom.

What was for her? That's a question that comes to me many days. Someone brings you into this world and you live with that person and then that person is gone; and even though you've had what felt like endless days with the person so you are full of that person's being—the voice and smell and touch—the person is a mystery. Or what accompanied the person is a mystery. You can say that each of us is followed by a penumbra of longing, but the longing my mother carried was different. It was as if she needed another language. Or she needed to be able to use language that no one much used. She would sit there with a glossy magazine and say, "That's beautiful" or "Isn't that something?" but the words felt fragile and pointless. Even when she said them to someone, she was more talking to herself. She was dreamy, but there was no dream to move toward. There were no blues for her to sing. She hummed a few hit parade songs like "Tennessee Waltz," which I mentioned already, sometimes singing the words in a sweet, quiet voice. My sister said, much later, that our mother had been "depressed"—one of those words that makes something personal into something impersonal.

When my mother started to get sick from cancer, she was very calm, as if she expected to die before she reached sixty, as if that was part of the plan. She talked to me on the phone and didn't seem any sadder from the illness. Maybe the illness was a relief. She didn't have to put on a show; pity got on her nerves. No one knew the depth of feeling in her, so why should anyone pity her? She would say, "I felt funny this morning when I got up. Something's off." What I felt was that more was off than she could ever say or I could understand. That's how the world was: "off."

* * *

Words for her were more like sighs—
Smiles were little schemes—
Her good days waved—then drifted by—
Love was one more dream.

My first tool of liberation was a beige transistor radio. I lay in bed at night and listened to the world beyond my town. I had no idea what was out there. Why would I? That little plastic electronic box opened up my head.

The better-known music worlds were for parents: show biz smoothies, nightclub singers, big bands, Your Hit Parade, and a winsome sea of sentimentality. What I tuned into—country music and black music—were apart. There wasn't much money to be had from poor whites and poor blacks. Record companies in New York and Los Angeles could make or break acts, but people still performed on their local radio stations. The America that interested me was still local.

Every station had its own disc jockeys, which meant many of them had the chance to play what appealed to them. They could be enthusiastic, whimsical, and knowledgeable. Elvis, after all, got going because a local disc jockey recognized something very special was happening. As I lay there, a form of magic was at work spinning sound filaments through the darkness. The DJ voices cackled, brayed, soothed, emoted, joshed, exclaimed, and declaimed but never mumbled. They not only were present in their words; they reveled in their words.

Shreveport, Nashville, Saint Louis, Memphis, Chicago, the signals went searching into the American night. I knew they were cities—workaday places—but they seemed mythical. The ads and jingles for cars, colas, and Preparation H to relieve hemorrhoids couldn't disperse that immense feeling. I was where I wanted to be: elsewhere. The black and white of America began to become real to me, providing shots of rhythm and blues and twanging country harmony. If I had no one to tell about what I was listening to, that was all right. I liked the music as my own possession and secret. Whatever the music was telling me—mostly about men and women having their problems getting along, though just as often in praise of womankind—was for me to learn.

I kept hearing someone named Jimmy Reed. The subjects were the usual—his boss, Mississippi, his woman's ways—but the music had this gait to it, rolling yet taking its sweet time.

The bass line felt unstoppable, a moving, magnetic force. I loved the acoustic blues, but his guitar was electric dynamite. He may have sung South, but he played urban. The great artists know both sides of the tracks.

Those songs of Jimmy Reed or Muddy Waters or Howlin' Wolf carried a deep sex charge. Thick and sensuous, the music strutted and bragged, the full force of what Muddy called "a mannish boy." Pop songs fetched a notion or metaphor and spun it out like so much cotton candy. You did the spinning and you had a song: white guys crooning nothings. That was not the way of Jimmy Reed. His feeling came from the blues—shrewd and resigned at the same time—but the pace was up-tempo and the sound stung. Something had been freed in America.

What black people got back for what they created was another question to which I had no answer. The music I heard, like Jimmy Reed, didn't live in my town. I could imagine towns and cities where he was on the jukebox, but I couldn't imagine the world his music came from. Beyond what was going on in my head, I didn't come from a sound-world. Jimmy Reed's music was his, but it felt shared, like something people partied to and danced to and got drunk to. That could have been my long-distance longing for some real fun, some juice. Something was there that was important not just to hear but to live. The music was an attitude: You better live now, because you don't get it back.

Even at a distance, I had to wonder where white people got off telling black people about anything; not only were they wrong, they were laughable. The white world that I delivered each morning in the newspapers was supposed to matter, but Jimmy Reed was what really mattered. When my dad would hear me out about one of my cockeyed complaints—Jimmy Reed versus Dwight Eisenhower—he'd say, "Well, Abe, I guess that's the way you see it." And it was. And Jimmy Reed was my president.

The white side of the street was led by Hank Williams, who could go in opposite directions: upbeat sometimes—"Hey, Good Lookin'"—but other times bereft—"I'm So Lonesome I Could Cry." When Williams was down, he was keening from some place far beyond heartbreak. I didn't want to learn where that was, but his voice pulled me in. I didn't have the word back then, but that voice was vulnerable. I was studying to be a man, studying the poses, so that was not what I wanted to be, yet his voice called to me. As they say, it had my name on it. You couldn't listen and not be touched.

I lay there in my bed with its knotty pine headboard while musical giants kept me happily awake. Who would have known from the TV's news, so sure of its official importance, that so much feeling was alive and well in the USA? Out there in the free-for-all night, the disc jockeys were fast-talking their way through the small hours: "My man, Jimmy Reed, he's tops at any speed! 45 or not, the man is hot!" In my room's closed-door darkness, I snugged my little music box by my left ear. I'd slowly move the wheel of the AM channel dial—its edge had small notches so the dial wouldn't slip—and pull in yet another "groove that's gonna move you."

• • •

Looking for a joy ride south—
Waiting on a song—
Heaven opening, soft then loud—
That note where I belonged.

In school I filled up notebooks with doodles and sketches and bits of poems. I'd sit there and the teacher would be telling us something about science or geography or history, and I'd think, How does she know? and Why does she care? If I had said that out loud, I would have been pegged as a wise guy, a delinquent, to use a word favored back then—which inside me I was. My role was to pass through the knowledge factory and receive those explanations about light waves and paramecium and the Missouri Compromise. I slouched and stewed, daydreaming about songs and girls. I looked forward to the bell. Let me out!

My quarrel was with the inability to let things be, whether glorious or inglorious, candy or spinach. Instead, there was this trail of talk behind everything. When people ask me questions about my songs—"How did you come to write this?" or "What does it mean?" or "Are you influenced by?"—a red light goes off in my head. Most college-educated people have a rage for explanation, for getting to the seeming bottom of things. My rage is against explanation. I don't think there is any bottom. Human beings do what they do. Many books are written, but you can't explain Hitler or Christ or Patsy Cline or—to bring it back home—Abe Runyan. They happened.

Supposedly, the explanations console us by cutting the

mysteries and dilemmas down to size. Atheists would explain to me how people needed to invent God. Political people would explain how the working class needed to be duped. Folk singers would explain to me how one version of a song was more real than another. More real! I tried to listen but never got very far. I'd blurt out something along the lines of "You don't mean that, do you?" They'd look at me. "Damn right I mean it, Abe. Don't you understand, Abe?" I didn't, and I don't.

My dad offered me his version of explanation, a father's task, the lump sum of male experience. I'd ask him about how people treated other people and he'd offer one of his apothegms: "That's the way the cookie crumbles," or "That's life in the big city." He might smile a scrap of a smile. He might sigh. He might start talking about a truck the company needed to buy but couldn't afford. He might leave the room—on to his next task. However well-meaning, his words did nothing so much as piss me off. I wanted to say, "You don't mean that, Dad, do you? You're my father. You've got to have more inside you than phrases." He read the newspaper each day and he read about the Civil War, especially about the Minnesota First Volunteer Regiment and Gettysburg; but after the smoke of paragraphs, stories, reports, and interviews vanished, there were, on the other side of too many words, too few words—the pit of resignation.

It wasn't as though I didn't want to get along myself, listening to what got said, believing that everything—the internal combustion engine and Korean War and Brylcreem — made sense. I could sign on: how the universe feels designed for each of us, a lukewarm bath that's there every day. The big questions, such as why are we here and what are we doing, would feel not so big. What, after all, do we know? Enough to be dangerous. No wonder I gave the reporters a hard time. The strayed, the sleepless, and the shaken are my audience, not the explainers.

Songs aren't explanations. Songs are lyrics—praising life for being life. It's the basic category and goes on forever: songs about frogs, sunsets, railroad engineers, and cowgirls named Jane. Some songs, not just mine but people like Kurt Weill, for instance, come at an angle. You could say those songs are trying to undo the explanations: You think you understand, but you don't. The lyric part is still there; people are raising their voices. Mack the Knife, though, is a person. He doesn't explain anything. He lives his life.

I remember a famous bluesman saying that the person who taught him to play was his stepfather—"a better player than I'll ever be but never recorded." He shook his head and said his stepfather was "lost in the sands of time." Not too many of us like to hear about those sands, but that seems what mostly happens. We forget, which is a blessing. If we consciously carried every indignity, we'd all be jumping out windows. If we act as if explanations banish the obscurity and uncertainty, though, that's a lie. A bluesman would understand that. That's some of what the blues is about: You can try to explain but you can't, and it doesn't matter anyway. The train pulls out of the station.

I sound like my father. Life's always biting me in the ass that way. I'm seeking a way out and there is none, except for my songs, which aren't so much ways out as ways further in.

In the songs, making sense and not making sense play tag. They're alleys and paths that don't go anywhere in particular and don't have to. They don't have to explain themselves.

Why were you born? Why does the sun come up in the morning? Why do you love someone one day and not love that person the next day? When you start coming up with explanations, you're bound to move away from the feeling of being here. Whatever the feeling is—happy or sad or in between—it's present the way that if you want to cool off on a hot day, you jump in a Minnesota lake. That's what I've been doing, over and over, making that jump. There's an expression my mom used where you say that you sold something for a song. It means you sold it cheap, but it's the opposite to me. What's cheap are explanations. They come and go. They're reasonable wind. They never have an answer for a song because there is none.

• • •

Boy at a desk considering a wall—
Boy with a question or two—
Words drifting through the dusty air—
Truths that can't be true.

When rock 'n' roll came along, the sound was like the crackle of a fire turned into music. Any teenager who wasn't afraid of his or her body was bound to be moved. Even if you were afraid of your body, the music could start you quaking. You might not want to, but the power—the command of rhythm—was imperious.

Some cornballs like Bill Haley made a splash, but the real musical phenomena—Buddy Holly, Chuck Berry, and Little Richard, to name some of the best—were more like tidal waves. The jukebox at the town soda fountain, a place kids gathered after school, rarely got a rest. We sat in booths and bragged and flirted and gossiped and whispered; in love with our pulses and sometimes in love with someone else. In the background would be "Peggy Sue" or "Maybelline" or "Good Golly, Miss Molly." Men sang, but women ruled.

What we were listening to was, in the euphemism of the time, "young people's music." That was something new. The big bands my parents liked had appealed to young people, but the music wasn't "novel," to use a word my mom favored. She meant the electric guitar. Out of what seemed like nowhere, this instrument appeared that was radically different from the brass of the big bands. When I heard the big bands on records, they sounded ancient. I knew they were supposed to be hot, but they didn't sound hot.

The guitar was personal (guys had names for their guitars) but mounted a sound that cut through you yet had you dancing. The bands needed all those instruments joining in. A rock 'n' roll band seemed not so much a band as an all-out guitar attack. The big bands felt airy to me, everybody swaying to the musical breeze, but rock 'n' roll stung like a tribe of bees. It didn't hurt, though. Your nerve endings started clapping.

Those three people I named were very different from one another, and that told you something about the music's range. The songs weren't pop in the tunesmith sense. Chuck Berry was one witty, sharp, playful guy, but he was coming from the guitar place. The words matched the guitar—"like ringing a bell." Something broke loose in his songs, something slyly innocent, and in the songs of others. Buddy Holly sounded so sincere and fresh. Little Richard sounded so outrageous, shrieking for joy. Whoever they were and wherever they came from—the hi-my-name-is-Elvis-Presley-and-I'd-like-to-cut-a-record circumstances—didn't matter. Their music was a sign, one more Great American Awakening. Although the record companies did their best to temper the rough edges, rock 'n' roll offered sheer anarchy—the howling, gyrating, hormonal, pagan body meeting the electric needle of sound. Whatever was deadening to the spirit, what used to be called "conformity," rock 'n' roll opposed. The body was a spirit.

I'd see articles in the paper where ministers down South burned records: sinful music, devil music, which only made me like it the more. The jukebox stood in a very wholesome place—we're talking saddle shoes, long skirts, and ponytails—but there was something outlaw about those 45s. Everyone was supposed to know their place, especially Negroes, but here were some people who didn't seem to know their place and didn't care. What place was Little Richard supposed to occupy? He was zipping around in his own ether.

Any guy with any musical intention was bound to pick up a guitar and start trying to rock, but playing was harder than I thought. The chords were nothing remarkable. You could buy a teach-yourself book, but the timing and intensity and then the putting the music together in a band were challenges. I listened to the records—I had a decent ear—and practiced, but I was clumsy. I hadn't soaked up the rhythm. You can't fake that. The rhythm has to get into you if anything good is going to come out of you, and the rhythm was black and white, the basic American complexity.

I had fun, though, thrashing around with my buddies. Just looking at my Sears Roebuck guitar made me glad, much less trying to play it. I was part of something that went along with who I was—a broody, intense kid who knew from early on that he was going to have to move on. I wanted to become a rock 'n' roller like Buddy Holly but had no idea where that might take me. When Buddy died in a plane crash, I had an awful feeling, not just sadness for his death—he was so full of bouncy feeling and didn't seem much older than I was—but sadness for the fact of his going from one town to another in small planes, the ordeal of it. I wanted to leave, but I didn't know if I wanted to do that.

As it happened, I've spent my life looking out airplane windows. I tell people I'm good with it, but the going from here to there is not that simple. Touring, being on the road, is a kind of task: If you want people to hear you, you have to go to them. On that account I've envied writers. Your pages go into the world, and that's it. Many times when I'm up in the sky, I've thought about that crash, not so much being morbid as haunted. I can see, as if it were yesterday, the picture of the wreckage. I tell myself that if you aren't haunted, what are you doing here? Hundreds, if not thousands of flights, and my wondering, "Is this the time?"

My mother, who monitored me the way moms monitor their kids, considered the guitar I bought with some of the money I earned pushing a broom around my dad's truck garage "a phase I was going through." That was fair. Strutting a guitar was something guys did before joining the workaday parade. Music wasn't any kind of regular life. I felt, though, that if I dug in enough, the music would take care of me. I had a kind of blind faith. I wanted to not just live with those sounds but live in them. Even when I turned to the acoustic guitar and put the electric one away, that sound remained with me. I could hear Buddy Holly in my head, urging me on. He had been so alive.

. . .

Man searching a woman's sweet name—
Looking to speak desire—
Man waiting on a wayward shore—
Love lost to its own fire.

My grandmother Reva, who lived in one of the four bedrooms on the second floor of our house, loved mirrors. Each day Reva diligently fussed over her appearance. Since she had washed up on the shores of our little town after one divorce, one widowhood, and one husband who ran off ("a real no-goodnik"), she didn't have a big social calendar, but that didn't deter her. As she liked to say, "You have to keep up." Or, as my mother put it, "Reva is a vain woman." That was true but Reva didn't hoard her vanity. She shared it. Each bedroom had a large mirror that was a gift from Reva. One day I came home from school to find an ornate mirror attached to the back of my bedroom door. Around the edge of the frame, intricate leaves were carved in the dark brown wood. Reva told me they were acanthus leaves, as if that might mean something to me. It cost some money and must have come from what Reva called "the old country," wherever that was. "Use it in good health," Reva said to me—one of her favorite expressions that could apply equally to eating prunes, wearing wool scarves, and getting a new baseball mitt.

When you're a kid, mirrors can surprise you. You're so busy answering to others that you barely have a sense of being someone who can appear in a mirror. Is that me? Reva's mirror was lying. There was so much going on in me, yet my reflection showed nothing but a pudgy, curly-headed dope who needed braces.

That changed. The wonder of self-consciousness took hold the way it takes hold of most teenagers. Others notice you while you're noticing them—a risky business. Sometimes I wanted my insides to be expressed on my outside. Other times, I wanted to be hidden and private. I remember when I discovered sunglasses; I couldn't get enough of them. I'd wear them outside in the dark of winter. "You'll break your neck, Abe," my father would say.

The glasses made me a hipster, a term I was vaguely aware of. I didn't actually know anyone like that. Living in our town automatically meant you weren't a hipster. You were a hick, a hayseed, though the kids in town looked down on the kids in the countryside as being exactly that. For me, though, the distant look was worth cultivating. I could be where I was but not be there. No one could see in.

In my bedroom, in front of Reva's acanthus-leaf mirror, I'd try on poses. I was a guitarist, but you didn't just play a guitar. That was only part of it. You had to develop a sense of carrying it when you weren't playing, holding it between songs. You wanted to be natural yet professional. I had no idea what either was, but that was the benefit of the mirror, which helped me study. Whether I could play in some of the poses in which I saw pictures of Chuck Berry, crouched over and duck-walking, for instance, was unlikely. Still, it was something to shoot for there in my going-nowhere bedroom. I could be transported, which I've always counted as a plus.

I did a lot of facial posing too. I worked on my leer, my snicker, my blasé I-don't-care-in-the-least stare, my world-weary smile. No gush need apply: I was fortifying myself. If I was ridiculous, if you happened upon me and wondered if I was in something like my right mind, I'd have answered, "Too bad." I felt I had a lot to hold myself to, even if I wasn't sure what it was. I was certain that James Dean had stood before a mirror in his time. He had made himself into someone else, the way actors did. It took practice; the change didn't just happen. You had to get the poses down before you announced yourself to the world as someone else. You had to manage your self.

You don't go telling people about your secret self. It wouldn't be secret if you did, though secrets don't have to be dark. Secrets can be perfectly regular and day-lit, as in "I want to go somewhere and do something I like." You kept such secrets to yourself because your classmates in high school were ready to make fun of you for any discernible reason, though they didn't need a reason. Your existence was enough. Declaring what was going on inside your self would be a very bad idea. Posing was okay because it communicated something was happening, but there was no telling what that was. If this sounds anthropological, it was.

Was I vain like Grandma Reva? You could say that, but I was trying to make myself real to myself, so how a shirt collar looked when I turned it up mattered. I also was acting out various psychodramas in front of the mirror. Here's Abe talking to Cathy, the girl in his homeroom whose body drives him crazy. Abe's coming on to her, but easy and cool. Here's Abe standing before an adoring crowd and taking the applause as a matter of fact. Here's Abe walking away from his house and his town, head down, determined. Does he see where he's headed? Does he care? He cares a very great deal, but he's not going to tell you. He's going to scowl and look aside and shake his head because he has better things to do. A mirror has told him so.

. . .

Face on a glass show me a sign—
Tell me how to get home—
Look back—look twice—look past these words—
Then you can be alone.

On account of dad owning a trucking business, I heard constant talk about how far one place was from another, always a distance because that was the Upper Midwest—space that went on forever, places that always seemed a few hundred miles from where we lived. You came to take the distances for granted. The drivers would joke about going for a day's toot— six hundred miles round-trip.

If you grow up in a big city, you understand the jostle and rush of American life, but you're going to miss the nation's essence—those big empty spaces. The farms where I grew up that dotted the countryside were outposts, little glimmers here and there at night, pieces of a broken necklace. The feeling of nighttime driving was overwhelming—so much darkness, so few people. Dad joked about wolves. Mom told him to be quiet.

I've spent my life trying to fill that emptiness. That sounds grand, perhaps, the existential palaver of a sensitive son of the middle border, but that's been my instinctive goal. I've been workmanlike at it. The emptiness became part of me when I was growing up. The questions were simple: What are people doing here? What am I doing here? No one was going to answer them for me. The answer the world gave was to not ask such questions, to put your head down and keep busy. We filled the emptiness with the bravado of our endeavors. Trucks whizzed down highways; drills attacked mountains of stone; freighters loaded and unloaded, winches groaning and dollies creaking: The soundtrack of American labor was endless. Back in the nineteenth century, that aural hurly-burly had filled Walt Whitman with awe.

I didn't think of the emptiness as good or bad so much as the basic fact that you were going to go forth to meet whatever was out there. How you carried yourself was something like a paradox. There was the disproportion between your human doings and the breadth of the emptiness. You were never going to take its measure. From the start, my efforts were futile, but that spurred me more than discouraged me. No

matter how much you raised your voice, your song in the wind
didn't travel very far. There was the feeling of the spaces' indifference, how they swallowed you up. That made the doings
all the more poignant: Yodeling into the abyss, a folksinger
friend once put it.

The good news of my situation lay in the endless trove of
inspiration. To me, out there where I grew up, every destiny in
America spoke to the emptiness. Huck Finn, Hester Prynne,
Captain Ahab, Gatsby and Daisy, Holden Caulfield, they all
seemed on the same semi-eloquent page to me, all trying to
fill in the blank, inner miles. When in high school I read *On
the Road*, Jack Kerouac's adventures seemed natural. He got it,
about the emptiness. He was as much a car as he was a person—an American dilemma. He was hectic, but he was keen
to the loneliness. The questions that bugged me bugged him.
His answer seemed to be to keep moving, which made sense.
If you settled down, you were bound to succumb to your days'
narrowness, your life as a closet. You filled in the vastness with
your propulsion, wrongheaded or not.

Behind the emptiness was terror. Though that was the
hardest thing to acknowledge, the crawling feeling inside
me, what else could have been there? My first inclination—
the aspirin of self-preservation—was to crack a joke. Many of
my songs do that—amuse about the terror. Humor gives you
a handhold on what can't be grasped. That only went so far.
Anyone who was mildly alert understood how the emptiness
could steal your soul away. Your instincts and knowledge were
worthless. Your amiable anecdotes didn't matter. Your money
was laughable. Your politics were scrawny and pitiful. You

could pretend as an American that you knew what you were doing, but that was only pretend.

Living with the terror is an ordeal, like something from a Poe story or Ahab on the boat. Everyone wants you to minimize it, to offer some reassurance. In that way, music is an industry like any other. The songs are glimpses and snatches you can enjoy for your listening pleasure, but they are somewhere you visit. The person who makes the songs, however, the songs that probe and dwell, the songs that acknowledge the price of the ticket, that person can tell you, if you care to hear, that there is no heart of emptiness. There is only this terrific, gnawing meaninglessness. Whatever answers I've proposed weren't answers. They were more like echoes.

You have to make your own way through it, which was easy to say but hard to live. More than once, I thought of the guy in the myth who used string to find a path through a labyrinth. The emptiness, though, was formless. You could point to the night sky above the land. You could point to the land itself, but there were no consoling definitions. You had to make them up on your own, which meant you had to feel how flimsy they were. Only the people who lived here before the white people had definitions that had been tested. Everyone knew what happened to them. What wisdom they'd accrued was pushed aside, mocked or condemned.

Tell us it ain't so, Abe. Tell us you can fill up the emptiness. Or, better yet, tell us there is no such thing, that it's a figment of imagination, a crotchet, a point of despairing pride, something that worldly confidence can blow aside like so much dandelion fluff. I'd nod because I heard and understood. The terror wasn't of my making. Even the songs I made weren't of my making. They issued from something much larger than I was. I'd been down that nowhere highway. I'd looked and listened. I'd been properly spooked. I could talk smart, but I'd been spooked. When a critic accused me—as only a critic could put it—of "imaginative indigestion," I half-agreed. I was lucky I didn't choke. More than once, I almost did.

. . .

Went past a town but missed its name—
Then another there—
In between, land like sky—
Days so unprepared.

If you had looked for Abe Starker on a Saturday afternoon in the early 1950s, you would have found him at the Grand Theater on Main Street watching Westerns. Gary Cooper, Walter Brennan, Alan Ladd, Robert Mitchum, and John Wayne were as real to me as my parents. In a way more real, because for two hours I gave myself up to each explicit movie moment. My parents were a separate reality—here long before I came along. They might tell stories (usually overheard), but their inner histories were impenetrable. In the dusty cow towns and barrooms and stagecoaches, I was alerted to decisions that meant dying or living: the endgame of right versus wrong. The gunfighters' rises and falls left me rapt, but I thrilled, too, to the vagaries of justice and injustice. Every Western was a fable.

I knew the weight and pace of each scene, the inevitable unfolding as when the sheriff—a tall, thin man whittled by virtue—walked slowly to a gunfight where lifetimes would play out in a blink. You'd see his measured steps, one after the other, his boots moving forward but in no hurry. Destiny was not going to swerve; there was no need to rush. When someone got excited—talked fast or ran—you felt how something had gone wrong. Fools babbled because they didn't hear the tread of fate.

The bad guys were masters of contempt. Carefully, they doled out scorn, to say nothing of loathing. A turning of the head or spitting into the dust or readjusting a hat made plain a long tale of hard feeling. The bad guys knew—or so it seemed to me—they were going to lose, but they gave the good guys a run for their righteous money. They could cause some suffering: Innocent people would die because there were no innocent people. As for the women, they were measured at times—trying to talk sense to men—and unmeasured at others—yelling or crying because of what men had done. They were kites at the mercy of the wind.

Inevitably, death—via six-shooter or rifle or lynch mob—rankled the air. The nation was not very old, but vivid memories of the murdered—Indian and settler alike—clouded the open, western skies. America was drenched in violence; the compromises that talk promised were futile. Blood had to be shed. The triumph of order was meant to placate, but that triumph felt like something you had to accept more than you had to like. The outlaws were ever looking for shortcuts—robbery, for instance—that threw off the orderliness. Who wanted to root for the banks? Who didn't find the town prostitute more interesting than the town preacher?

As in my town, the Westerns had types. The sheriff was stoical. He had lost someone or something and was making up for it. Or he was trying to live up to some ideal—who his father had been—or right some wrong he'd suffered—who his father had not been. The sheriff was invincible—he wore a badge—but he wasn't. He had a flaw. He believed in other people too much or refused to listen to them at all. He took everything on himself or he trusted someone who was deceitful. In any and all cases, he said little. His gun did the talking.

The main bad guy was the flip side of the sheriff—a full-of-himself braggart, far from invincible but capable of very accurate shooting. On both sides there were sidekicks, lesser mortals doomed to lesser vision, who were neither heroes nor antiheroes. They perished in the various fracases because they were obviously expendable. Also present were the onlooking townspeople: the newspaper editor, the saloonkeeper, the gambler, and, above all, the women—standing by their men, living statues clutching their sewing or a child's hand or a plate, praising and lamenting, ever watching, their eyes haunted by the passion of their dependent lives.

An unreal world, a pointlessly moral world, a wrong-headed world, a falsely mythic world. My words mock me because whatever it was, I—the eleven-year-old munching popcorn and Raisinets—adored it. The rudiments of drama spoke, and I heeded them. People were not going to get along: settlers and Indians, deputies and outlaws, schoolmarms and truants, bankers and robbers. Those were categories, but the disagreements ran deeper. Some people were good; some people were evil. Those words might not come out of mouths, but there they were. Nor could either side do much about it. A wife might plead with her husband that he didn't have to face the murderous gunfighter. The gunfighter might muse about how he'd once been a boy with nothing more on his mind than doing his chores on the farm back in Ohio. Fortune, however, hovered nearby: You become this, not that. The outcome was frightening but exciting too. Everyone went through the same wringer.

I watched the stubborn sheriff who knew he was walking into an ambush. "I know you're there," he would say. Being good, he was wounded but lived, unlike the bad guy, who died writhing on the ground and was given a few last words, sometimes repentant, sometimes proudly impenitent. In the background, untouched and endless, loomed this panorama called "The West," a landscape I'd never visited in so-called reality. My imagination, however, had entered a promised land.

The Westerns were not just larger than life but something time had perfected, every scene an imperative ritual. I didn't see myself with a holster and hat. I, who shied away from playground fights, doubted how brave I was. Nor did I see myself as a noble Indian speaking sagely as my way of life was destroyed through greed, lies, and hatred. For sure I wasn't wise, much less noble. And the Indians in the movies were more known for their perishing than anything. What I wanted was for my steps to resound like the sheriff's, slowly pacing the dusty street or wooden sidewalk. I wanted to hear my unmistakable self.

. . .

Gave the wicked some room, bowed to the good—
Hell came by for tea—
Stood firm on ground that wasn't mine—
Writhed in the mortal sea.

When you come up through the musical ranks, when you are finding your way to the music, when the music seems to descend on you—gradual and sudden, common and remarkable as nightfall—when you start to become aware of how nowhere you are and how somewhere the music is and how you desperately want to get there, then you start to get a small clue about who is speaking to you through the long-playing spin of the years: the dead, the uncountable forebears whose notes and words inform each strumming day.

As a kid, you take every day as if it was made for you—"comin' right up"—the way a waitress at the local diner would holler down the counter at some gent holding up his empty coffee cup, her voice full of come-and-get-it life. But the days weren't all there for the taking. Fate or God or Whatever You Wanted to Call It doled them out, and you probably did poorly by them. My ancestors' songs were in my head too—the wailing of repentance, the Jewish blues. Once when I was visiting one of my mom's brothers, it was Yom Kippur; we went to the synagogue and I heard it for myself, that long thin line of perishable sound.

Few names were attached to the past's voices. On that account—all those ballads written by "Anonymous"—I've done my share of impromptu and solitary cemetery visiting, witnessing how the names and epitaphs and dates have faded in the rain and snow and sun, how remembrance has become illegible. Standing there before a tombstone, I try to see a person who once was walking and talking, thinking and forgetting, tying a shoelace and eating an apple.

Being with the graves has soothed more than it has agitated. Those rows of final facts are staring at you as much as you are staring at them—the mystery of done and gone, another matter that the blues guys got right. What they had to hold onto—a shack, a mule, a guitar—could be taken at any instant. Death, though, took everyone. If your life always had to go scraping through the back door, always on the wary alert, there was satisfaction there. Some important white person would kick the bucket and you knew, though they would never speak to you, that all the other high and mighty folks could do was shake their heads and sputter clichés.

For the names on the stones to fade can take centuries, but oblivion is in no hurry. We're in a hurry because we live with a calendar. We need to keep track of the days, I get that; but there's no real keeping track of the days. More than one of my songs is about that—the no keeping track. "Gone" is one of my favorite words. The days admonish and advise—on Tuesday there will be a test, a bill that's due, an appointment with the doctor—but the pool of time we're paddling around in has no form. When a volcano blows or an earthquake happens, the calendar has nothing to say. The vastness—earth, stars, galaxies—goes by its own time.

A person—the accounting of finite years—could get seriously rattled. I felt that even as a kid, how there was so much disappearance on the outskirts of life, people my parents referred to who were gone, plus the shelves and shelves of books in the library about so-called famous people who were gone. "Remember," my mother would say about someone who ran a grocery store or worked in a beauty parlor. My father would shake his head. He didn't remember. My mother would persist: "He was tall. She had red hair. I think she dyed it." Maybe my father would start to realize who the person was, maybe not. I sat there at the dinner table and pushed my canned peas around and sawed at my portion of flesh.

How could you not think that someday someone would say that about you? Remember Abe Starker, his father owned some company; he lived over on the west side of town? Or was it the north side? Remember Abe Starker, he won the fifth-grade spelling bee? He won on the word "indissoluble." What year was that? The gravestones protested, but most people stayed out of graveyards, especially in America, where the past was something to eliminate. "Over and done with," as my high school principal liked to say about anything he didn't want to talk to us students about. "Out, out," as Shakespeare put it.

I keep a notebook in which I write down the names on tombstones. I travel, so I have many names. I can hear my grandma saying, "Abe, you are a strange boy." But not really, because by writing down the names I am joining a living hand to a vanished hand. I sometimes take the notebook out from the bookcase where I keep it and pore over the names. I'm praying in my way to the immensity of everyone having once been here. I'm locating a version of holiness. I'm hearing the small ping of lost sound. I'm indulging my own queasy mortality.

Songs can honor that immensity. Some of the names in my songs—John Fuller and Amy Blake in "The Ballad of Confusion" (it has the refrain about the "availing rain")—come from the notebook. In school no one cared about the immensity. Everything was about "we did this and that important stuff in this and that important year, pilgrims and kings and scientists." Swell, but what about everyone else? What did each one of them do? Shouldn't there have been a few examples from that enormous category? Who cleaned the floor and raised the goat and baked the bread? I had to wait, but my songs have let me ask those questions. As for cemeteries, they were where you took girls to have sex. Or hoped to. You didn't bring a notebook with you.

. . .

Talking about time—slow or fast—
Kid had a big long head—
Went down the river, down the deep cave—
Spoke his life to the dead.

The following is an interview I conducted in my head, one of many.

So did Abe think of himself in the third-person?

—Yes.

And imagine he was being interviewed?

—In high school, yes. And afterward for a time. Then he started to be interviewed for real and discovered he didn't like being interviewed.

But back in his early carefree days—

—Saying they were "carefree" shows the problems that go with interviews—framing the narrative, glibness.

Let's switch things then. Did his family have a dog?

—A collie named Rex.

Did he love the dog?

—He wished his family had another dog so he could name that dog. He wanted to have a dog named Carlo. Who knows where he got that name from? But, yes, he loved Rex, though Rex seemed indifferent to his love. Rex's most avid tail-wagging was reserved for Abe's father, Max, who seemed to do the best job in the family of behind-the-ear scratching.

Well, it's never too late to scratch a dog behind the ear. Now, to switch the topic again, I've heard that Abe's been called a conservative. Is that a political designation?

—No.

How so then?

—He wants to take care of what's here: children, trees, dogs, songs. He doesn't want to fly with the arrow of time. He likes wheels, whatever goes round and round.

Does that put Abe in a different place from his progressive brethren?

—Brethren?

Answer the question, Abe.

—If you mean that most other people he knows tend to be more positive about where time is headed, the answer is "Yes." But he hasn't been one for prying under people's rocks, which interviewers often do. If you pry under a rock, you could find a snake. This is where Abe starts to lose patience and begins to show how fractious he can be.

Speaking of which, did he ever cry as a child?

—What kind of question is that? If you fall down as a child, you cry.

I mean beyond falling down. I mean crying because of emotional situations when he got older.

—Yes. That way, the not-falling way, he cried a few times. Mostly due to teenage heartache, being betrayed. He took love hard.

What did he learn from that?

—He learned to watch his heart. He wasn't good at it, though. He pretended he was, you know, acting as if love were for other people.

That seems a pointless pose.

—Well, you sound like the usual self-important interviewer who strikes an attitude when someone tells you the truth. May we move to a lighter topic, such as were there any goldfish in his house? Or what was his favorite TV show? Probably *Have Gun—Will Travel*. Paladin was another person he identified with. Or—to pose a larger question—did Abe think of himself as a moral agent? That's a good one; the answer to which is "No."

Thanks for the information, Abe.

—Anytime (though he doesn't mean that).

* * *

My words ran off—didn't come back—
People said I'd failed—
Their words stood tall like endless laws—
My tongue-tied mind was jail.

My parents wanted to have a family because that was what a man and a woman did—have a family. If there were any married couples in our town who didn't have children, there was some unhappy story in the background that my mother would whisper to another woman friend when they were playing gin rummy and drinking ginger ale about "she couldn't" or "they waited too long," or something similarly fateful. I can recall the women at the card table shaking their heads but then brightening up because they did have children. They were part of a family they had made. The notion of people not wanting to have children was not a notion but an exotic belief like the people were Zoroastrians or Rosicrucians.

Since I went ahead and had a family, I'm not one to talk, but I am one to talk. I agreed with the premise. You honored the life force. You wanted to share your devotion. You wanted to be a father or a mother. You wanted to complete the circle that your wedding ring showed you. I never asked them because you didn't ask your parents any questions back when I was growing up, but I think they felt the same way. No one ever paused and said, "Well, it's great we have these children, because once children are there, the uncertain drama of generational karma begins." It was more like "Did you brush your teeth? How many

times have I told you to brush your teeth?" Rules and reminders
fill up the rooms fast.

In the face of the elemental wind of what has to be done
next, appreciation is not a very strong candle. Maybe appreciation—time out to say I'm glad you're here—needs a space
families can't provide. Once there's birth, there's motion; the
longings, hopes, regrets, fears, desires, and resentments that
drive the days forward toward death. The feelings have to fend
for themselves. They turn quickly into anger: You could and
should have, but you didn't.

My parents loved me—my dad on the sly because he was a
guy and my mom gushier because she was a mom—but I felt
myself drowning in their expectations: Was I who they wanted
me to be or was I not? The Question of Abe hovered in the
air, as when I "forgot" to clean my room because I had other
things to do, such as listening to music, which went on for
hours and didn't seem to be doing much of anything, or when
I brought home a report card that had its share of Cs and typed
remarks like "Doesn't pay attention" or "Can't be bothered." I
can remember my dad frowning and my mom making a click-
ing sound with her tongue. "You can do better," they'd chorus
at me. I could; that was true. I didn't want to, though. What
I wanted was to be free. "Free" wasn't a family word. Families
were defined. I was a revel of indefiniteness: Jewish boy from
West Nowhere meets spirits of Robert Johnson, James Dean,
and Buddy Holly. Uncertain chemical reaction occurs; stay
tuned for improbable reports. I hemmed and hawed, made
excuses and fumed, made short-lived amends, and brought
home another round of Cs

There wasn't a lot beyond the highway and the sky for me to look out at and call "the world." What I knew—and could feel like the bite in the winter air—was that I wanted to be in that great hypothesis. My sister got married right after college, stayed in-state, and saw my parents every week or two. There were years when I didn't see my parents at all. My sister told me I was a "brat" for acting like that; but once I was out there in the real world, not the one in my head, I was lost and found at the same time, finding myself by making up myself. To walk again through the front door of the house I grew up in was to become lost all over again, to sink into a past I could do nothing about. Until I was sure I was found, I couldn't chance it. That took time.

My parents wanted me to do this and do that because that's what parents do: They have kids, and then they want. There's random joy and there's steady worry or, as my dad liked to say, "concern," as in "I'm concerned, Abe." With my own kids I tried to be calm and ask questions about what they were thinking, but I doubt if I did any better. As they got older and explained themselves to me, I heard the phrase "What were you thinking, Dad?" more than once.

My family didn't make me doubt myself. They wielded the sword of Jewish betterment and assumed that was what I wanted: college, a profession, a settled life. They took me seriously, but my seriousness had nothing to do with theirs. I left as a young man with some songs in his head. I could fall just fine on my own face.

. . .

Asked my mother to be my brother—
Asked my sis to hide—
Asked my dad to be more real—
They told me to play outside.

When I jacked off to a photo of Bridgette Bardot in a bikini or fantasized that she had a sister and I was in bed with both of them, or when I drank beers with guys even though we weren't the legal age to be drinking beers, or when I told my mother I was going to a guy's house to help him fix his bicycle but I was going to a girl's house to neck, a girl my mother disapproved of because she was poor and her father was in jail, I wasn't being something called "good." You pick up judgments as you grow up the way you attract lint. My parents never thundered. Most of my teachers never thundered. The newspaper was mute words. Yet I felt a hand on me every day, the hand of "be good."

I couldn't see what was bad about getting excited about Bridgette or my girlfriend or drinking a beer. I thought, as they say in America, it was all good, but the word didn't seem to apply. Could bad be good? Later I heard black guys say something was bad and they meant "good." I liked that, one more way that black people constructed their own sense.

No one in my daily rounds of school and home meant "good" in any serious sense like someone in the Holocaust who hid Jews and risked his or her life and was a good person for doing that. They meant neat, orderly, keep-it-clean, don't-make-trouble, stay-in-line. I can hear my grade school teachers saying that as we gathered to come in off the playground: "Children, now stay in line." We tended to be unruly, that was true. Lines were good if you wanted to enter the school in a respectful fashion and not like a bunch of little hellions. Did being in line have to be all of life?

I guess it did. When I stopped singing songs for various good causes, some people gave me serious grief. I wasn't being good. I was selfish. I was cynical. I was hopeless. Some simple answer on my part—as in, I wrote the songs and sang them and then I wanted to write some other songs and sing them— wasn't a sufficient answer. People had congratulated me and praised me for being good. How dare I stop being good? I had stood on the side of justice. I still thought I was standing on that side, but other people told me I wasn't.

One reason goodness exists is so people who feel they are good can tell off people who aren't good. When I read *The Adventures of Huckleberry Finn*, I felt how Mark Twain got that one. And when I read that Hemingway said American literature began with Huck Finn, I understood him. The American struggle isn't with evil; it's with goodness. America carries this terrible weight of goodness and wants to be applauded and loved for it, but no one asked America to carry that weight. No one asked the people around Huck to spend their lives telling him to stay in line while they were condoning slavery, because slavery was law and law was rules and rules were good and there was nothing more to say beyond "Be obedient." "Why should I?" Huck answered. He came, though, like my girlfriend, from a disreputable place. His answers didn't count.

It's not as though I liked walking around with the words "Bad Abe" pinned to my back the way in school we would pin a piece of paper to someone's back that said, "Kick me." But I felt how goodness would have killed me. That sounds drastic, but the feeling was drastic. I wasn't interested in making unnecessary trouble, but I was interested in being a body with a body's inclinations. Not every inclination might work out—going too fast on a motorcycle or injecting something into your veins—but that was for me to find out.

When fear becomes daily, it almost ceases to be fear, just another habit and one that goodness assuages because goodness is fear's antidote. I'm being good, so I'll be okay. I'll be safe and secure. Meanwhile there has to be more to living than being safe and secure. But meanwhile there are people who don't trust their pulses, people from the government who are talking about national security and defense (not war) and safety. What I hear is that they want to live in a box that is a good box because they know that box. And their box is better than the boxes other countries have. Their box is the best box. Keep your head down and your flag waving.

Then how about the department of insecurity? Where does that come in? I know—that's why there are these pills everyone takes. Shut up, Abe, and write your songs and make them good songs not some weird shit. Sing about love and puppies and flowers.

Love can sour, puppies shit on the floor, and flowers wither and die. Are those songs worth singing? "What do you want to go make trouble for?" my grandma would say to me when I left the house any high school evening in pursuit of some harmless pleasure. "Can't you be good? Can't you stay in your room and study your books?" Ah, the negatives that accompany goodness. Books were fine—that's where I found Huck— but I wanted to live like Huck and not just read about him. I'd close the front door and mutter. I wasn't going to hate myself or try to be someone else. If I wasn't virtuous, that's how it was. And really, if you're a grown person, someone who doesn't get tucked in every night, how can you be safe? Huck felt how goodness was the nation's chosen armor, how it wouldn't take yes for an answer, and how behind every lecture about being upright was an avenging paddle waiting to whop you.

. . .

He was good 'til he turned bad—
She was vivid but terse—
He angered fast but lost his aim—
Their love so unrehearsed.

Back in the 1950s when rock 'n' roll started to percolate out of the Southern earth, if you were from the North like me, you couldn't help but wonder about those places where the black and white of America lived side by historical side, segregated places, places of oblique horror and straight-out horror, but places, too, where music could seem stronger than laws and hatreds, where a mingling of joy and freedom arose, where "race music" ended and something new began. Little Richard, to choose one unforgettable I've already mentioned, was so free I sometimes couldn't believe him. Hearing his songs, I felt as if a secret universe was singing—playful, passionate, sound-crazy, dizzy, and glad of it. Richard Wayne Penniman was not on anyone's map—remember, Dwight Eisenhower was in the White House, one very white white man—but there he was. And people loved Richard. I sure did.

Like thousands of guys, I got an electric guitar (to go with the acoustic one and my folk side) and tried out rock 'n' roll. Rock 'n' roll was like that, sort of a drug, the feeling that you could stand up there and drive girls wild. All those girls in saddle shoes, skirts, and white blouses did their homework and went to church; but when Elvis stood up, they lost it. I wanted them to lose it for me.

In high school I was in bands and started bands and left bands and got kicked out of bands and, all in all, went nowhere, though I did learn to play in my fashion and stand up on a few stages—high school dances and Elks clubs—and feel plausible: Abe the very small-town rocker. As rocking went, it was a mild whiff. I was paying homage to something larger than myself and more real than myself. In my lurching, heady, blind way, I sensed that. You couldn't deny the sound of infectious joy.

As a matter of course, you could deny it. My parents, who did not agree on many topics (liberal mom, conservative dad), both felt that what Little Richard was doing was nothing more than screaming nonsense. When I told them there was a performer named Screamin' Jay Hawkins, they nodded, as if confirmed in their wisdom. What was the world coming to? Probably a question the Assyrians and Babylonians kicked around too, but I kept my world history opinions to myself.

What was the "screaming" about? Amid the jobs and the machines and the cities and the evening news and the daily caboodle and the weather forecast and the averted glances and all-purpose indifference—every dull, throttling reality—some people were wildly alive. As long as they could work out on a piano or rattle some pots and pans and raise their determined voices, they were happy to live in that musical moment. Many teenagers—a group who were neither children nor adults but who lived in their own physical, yearning, record-buying universe—needed to hear such voices, because when the voices came forward, their presence seemed immediately natural, as if they had been there all along, waiting to be heard, one more installment in the American legends department.

I suspected I was alive, but rock 'n' roll confirmed it. School told me I wasn't alive. Trying not to slouch at the dinner table while also trying to act interested in the local gossip told me I wasn't alive. Walking by myself at night down the dark highway that led nowhere told me I was alive but awfully sketchy, not much more than a sigh. There was no good reason for me to be here. I could have been elsewhere. I could have not been here at all. Those were big, unhappy thoughts to carry around, but I don't think I was the only kid carrying them around. When I was growing up after World War II, America turned its eyes outward toward all the stuff it could get its victorious hands on. No more mule and forty acres, no more sitting on the front porch shelling peas and watching the world go by. For better and worse, everything quickened. Rock 'n' roll was part of that quickening.

When I sat on the one chair in my bedroom and put my feet up on the desk and listened to Buddy Holly and the Crickets, I was communing with Buddy's bright voice, but I was communing with myself too. Something pure and unrehearsed was going on that I needed to know. Sure, it made me feel better—that was part of what I needed to know and feel—but it gave me a thread, also, to help me out of the do-as-you're-told rigamarole. The thread wasn't big or complex, but it was strong. The world would say, "It's only music. They're only songs," but I knew enough to distrust "only." That was a word people used when they wanted to push the truth away because the truth would upset their notions of what did and didn't matter. Buddy didn't set out to become the truth. He just did what he loved. That was how I wanted to live: doing what I loved.

After his death there were his voice and his songs. My parents would have called him another screamer (which was the last thing he was), while my friends who liked his music shook their heads when he died and said "too bad" and started talking about the dance on Saturday night or what was showing at the Grand. They already were on their way to somewhere else, the comfort of consecutive hours. I was too, but I wasn't going to forget the people who led the way. I was building a shrine inside me.

* * *

He got the twitch but left the itch
That's how his karma went—
Too many thoughts in idle hands
Guessing what meaning meant.

Back home, where I grew up, I never heard anyone say the word "artist." I certainly never heard a teacher say the word. Probably I first encountered the word on the radio when a disc jockey said, "recording artist." That sounded high-class, high-tone, not something from the dim, dime-store every day. The word gave off some gleam and stature. The word needed an adjective, though. The word wasn't strong enough to stand on its own.

What did the word mean? I could have been like one of the kids in English class who'd begin his or her theme with "According to *Webster's Dictionary* . . . ." Teachers ate that line up, but I wasn't that kid. Where in this world would someone say that word on its own, as in "Joe's an artist?" It beat me. People worked for a living—that was the beginning and end of everything. God had been the Big Worker, and everything came down from Him. He set the tone, but artists seemed to be people who didn't work for a living. Somehow a living happened for them magically. Or they starved. I'd read a novel about starving artists, but that was in France not Minnesota. They scrounged and got syphilis and died in the gutter. Horses pissed on their corpses.

A scary end, but I liked the notion of the word. I doubted if it would ever apply to me because the word was so vague, so likely to be bullshit pretension. I saw myself as a musicianer, as some of the Southern cats used to call themselves. I would write that down on my tax return, if I ever did a tax return. Still, as a word, "artist" could have some benefits. I told more than one girl in high school that I was planning to be an artist. That sounded good—she'd stop chewing her gum and look at me—until she asked what kind of artist. Oh, you know, a great artist. I made some airy, wry hand gesture at once indicating and dismissing my remarkable presence of mind. She'd give me the hairy eyeball and start chewing her spearmint again, but I could tell she had been impressed, however briefly. The word had ambushed her. The word came from my special place—elsewhere.

As to where I was headed, I knew that I wasn't going into business. I wasn't going to be a good person who helped people like a teacher or doctor. I sure as hell wasn't going to be a lawyer. I wasn't going to do something with my hands, because I wasn't very good with my hands. Good enough to play the guitar but not to become a carpenter. I could have driven a truck like the guys who worked for my dad, but I'd get bored. I fantasized about being a criminal, but I lacked resentment. As a way out, the word beckoned: over here, Abe, in the strenuous mists of the undefined.

I'd have to leave town to become such a person. Artists lived in big cities where there was so much going on that worthless people like artists could get by. I got a clue about that when I started hearing music by people called "folk artists." The phrase often appeared in the forest of notes on the backs of records. Once more, the adjective was butting in. I tried to picture banjo players in velvet jackets, but the people on the album covers looked earnest and clean-cut or old-timey in a work shirt and dungarees. The word was a noun but wasn't.

I'd have to make up my version. Being an artist had to have something to do with letting your imagination do the talking. Con men were called con artists, but I was aiming for more than sleight of hand via my mouth. There had to be connections that an artist made that other people did not make. That's why there were artists—to make those connections. My life, though, seemed to have no connections. Where I grew up was a dot on a large map. I learned to play the guitar on my own, picking and flailing in my bedroom. No Mister Chips type came my way in school. Despite the sky, the horizons were more shut down than wide open. All the connections were immediate, right in front of you, like picking up the morning paper and a cup of coffee. People loved their small talk. Did you hear, and I can tell, and that's a fact.

So I had a feeling that artists were people who somehow were otherwise, who had more to do than add their two cents to what their neighbors already agreed with. I imagined those people grandly or negligently called "artists" disagreed on principle, not out of perversity (though people accused me of that when I rearranged a song or revisited the chestnuts I grew up with) but because you couldn't learn anything or feel anything new unless you disagreed with the small talk. Politics was small talk; college was small talk; trying to get close to a girl was small talk. There was no such phrase as "large talk," but wasn't that what an artist was trying to do?

I was headstrong, maybe obnoxious and conceited, maybe only naive, maybe all the above. Who was I? That seemed the point, though. Who was anyone to become an artist in America? The word was suspect—people posing and drinking wine in art galleries and talking in probing tones about nothing—but the underlying endeavor was irresistible: Listen to my songs. The songs came from my own private wishing well, from someone who didn't know any better and didn't want to. Sometimes when my father would get mad at me for being moody and dreamy, he'd say that he'd like to put some sense in my head. I never said the word to him, but he was reading my mind: Wanting to be an artist was senseless. When I grew older and learned about men like Picasso and Dostoevsky or women like Georgia O'Keeffe and Bessie Smith, I learned that no one blessed them in the cradle. They had to make it up, and whether they were fearless or foolish and whether they thought of themselves as artists without any adjective or the word was irrelevant to them didn't matter. They made the forms that held the visions.

· · ·

Talked some big-shot words—some smalls—
Showed my name around—
Just a kid—just a drop of rain—
Someone more lost than found.

My favorite kind of book when I was a little kid was the tall tale. I couldn't get enough of them, especially Paul Bunyan, who came from where I grew up. He was imaginary, but he was a creature of the North Woods, and some of the stories about him hailed from my neck of the woods—like how he made a griddle as big as a pond with iron from the Mesabi Range and how he rolled that griddle across the state as if it were a hoop. When he told people to get out of the way, you could hear his voice in Colorado, and he was only speaking polite-like. When he shouted, the earth shivered and the sky started to rain.

He was part of the imagination that inhabited where I grew up, where the trees were bigger and winters longer and the sky went on until the middle of next week. He was part of America's boasting and bragging, but also imagining what it could be like to be free, so free nothing could contain you. Everything about Paul was abundant; nothing was tight or held back. His personality was like that too—generous and glad to help where help was needed.

One story outdid another: His sidekicks told tales about how high Iowa corn grew, or how a Montanan could look at a huge herd of sheep and know how many there were to the exact number, or how Texans preferred heat so that when a Texan who was working up in Michigan was thought to be dead from the cold and put in a crematory, he popped right up and said the heat suited him just fine. I loved the juice of those stories, the spunk, the fun of them. Through it all Paul was larger than life—a handy way to be.

I couldn't be Paul Bunyan, but I could tell tales. I could be a fabricator. I could get away in my imagination from where I was—bored silly at school or listening to my mom tell my dad about how so-and-so was sick or my dad telling my mom that work was busy but could be busier. Making up stories was my own protest movement. You could say it was not much more than lying, but I was interested more in making things up for the pleasure of making them up than in trying to dodge the truth. When I told people I did things I didn't do—playing in a band in California when I'd never even been to California—I was saving my precarious head. If I said I was born on a freight train, then I was born on a freight train. What mattered weren't a life's particulars but the sense of the particulars. What mattered was the feeling a person had for his or her life.

The impulse ran deep enough for me to change my name. I wasn't ashamed of my name—Abraham Starker—but I wanted another. I needed to become someone else. Or, more accurately, there was someone inside me who needed to come out and who needed another name. That need may seem weird, but writers change their names—Mark Twain, for instance—and musicians, such as Muddy Waters; actors and actresses commonly do it. You can hide out in another name, but also you can put forward a version of yourself that seems truer than the one you were born with—or at least fits better.

Names are arbitrary. My surname came from someone at Ellis Island who shortened my grandfather's long Russian name. In Yiddish the word means a tough guy, but I doubt if the official who gave out the name knew Yiddish. Or maybe he did. Maybe it was a kind of joke. I only knew my grandfather a little because he died when I was four, but he was a very mild man. Whenever I saw him, he gave me a quarter and winked at me. I wonder what he would have said when I became Abe Runyan. Wink at me probably. He had that reassurance of old people—been around more blocks than you can count.

I've been asked too many times about the last name I took. Sometimes I say that I wanted to be Paul Bunyan but that name already was taken, so I took one that rhymed with it. Mostly I say I read a writer once upon a time named Damon Runyon and liked him. He wrote about guys and dolls in New York, the Broadway world of gamblers and bootleggers and chorus girls. It couldn't have been farther away from where I grew up, but his language had a snap to it—"dead as last Tuesday"—that impressed me and stayed with me. And the names Nubbsy Taylor and Jew Louie and Baseball Hattie: Everyone was a character who had a hustle going. I could be a character too, and I could make up my own characters—Princess Marie and Half-Face Joe and the Snow Girl—and songs to go with them.

It's natural with any name to think of the rhymes that go with it. People who know me call me "Onion." Even my sister took to calling me that. She'd call up and ask for "Abraham Onion" and laugh her head off.

My name is like a solid whim, a nod to the stage within me, but the name I should have taken came from Paul Bunyan's crew: Shanty Boy. He never had a home and had forgotten his real name. He could sing any song and could—I remember this exactly from the childhood book—"make up words and music you never heard in this world." That was my man.

· · ·

The heaven-sent stories collapsed—
I'd have to write my fate—
The crucial actor fell asleep—
The watchman came too late.

Feeling alone can make you feel how singular you are and how pointless resistance is. The aloneness I've carried around with me has been a hole in my soul's pocket but has been my companion too, helping me stand aside, keeping my eyes and ears alert. In childhood I felt the weight of the winter nights, the sensation that the darkness wasn't going to end, that a blanket had been pulled over me unlike the ones on my bed, a blanket that was never coming off. I could trust in the sunrise the way anyone trusted, the way even—or especially—a child trusted, but that trust could feel more like weariness. I'd look out at the night beyond my bedroom window and wonder about it, about the darkness. How was the winter night part of my being here? What was it saying to me? I'd lie there and feel my body in my bed in the night, how I was located but I wasn't located. I could have been floating above the houses and trees, heading toward the moon, helpless, as much a spirit as a person.

My day-by-day companion in aloneness was Blackie, my mother's cat. My mom insisted on having a cat even though my father said they weren't clean. "Cleaner than you," my mother would reply and laugh. During the day Blackie came in and out of the house as he pleased. At night, he settled down, sometimes on my bed. He'd curl up and fall fast asleep. When he woke, he'd yawn as if he still could use more sleep. He'd lie there and start to feel how he was a cat. He took it from there.

I wanted to love Blackie the way my mom did, but he scared me, how unto himself he was. I wanted him to be interested in me, but he wasn't. He went his little way through the days and nights and was fine with that, keeping an eye out for the dog and sitting on the windowsill in the dining room and watching the robins or jumping every once in a while onto my dad's lap, as if to say, "I'm cleaner than you are. I groom myself every day." He knew things people didn't know. For starters, he knew how to be alone. He didn't need a tribe or a nation or a corporation. He never signed on any dotted lines. He was perfectly there but unorganized.

Sometimes, when I've been weak or down, my aloneness has asked for sympathy. That was wrong. You can't share aloneness. The old blues guys stressed the basics, namely that you go down alone. You may have friends, lovers, Cadillacs, and bank accounts, but you go into the ground in your own box. Nothing sad about that, nothing to be regretted: Each of us is one body not a bunch of them. Being one especial body is part of our dignity; my aloneness isn't yours, nor can you borrow the dignity of that aloneness like a suit of clothes. The dignity lies in awareness, which means you can lose it. You can trade your aloneness for something bright but worthless, a trinket the world tosses you, and lose what dignity you may have had. For their own reassurance, people want you to be something other than you are and say something other than you feel. Easy to become a shell and keep talking. Happens every day.

Aloneness can give you strength—my life not yours—but aloneness can cut a person off. There's part of me that never has been close to anyone, including the women I've loved. There's part of me, first and last, that lives in my imagination. You can touch me, but I'm not there. Access isn't something I can pass out like tickets. There's something in me that's beyond me, something that seals me off but replenishes me. Call it the artist, call it the song maker, call it haunted. The names can only mean so much.

I heard the songs when I was growing up about sitting by the phone and waiting for a ring, and I heard Hank Williams singing about the lonesome whistle, but lonesomeness never has bothered me. I don't mean to play down the desolation behind lonesomeness, the feeling of no one caring, but desolation is the work of human beings, not the earth we live on. You can always go out for a walk and remember how the earth is your companion—there first and there after you. The trees and birds and rivers never created wars and prisons. I've gotten letters from guys doing time, and they write about the desolation, the being cut off. They're being confined. That's so hard—to be confined, to have no earth or sky.

We tend to go around looking for our missing parts, but no parts are missing. What's there is enough. You don't have to do any wanting. That could sound self-satisfied—Abe's mystify-the-interviewer, bullshit wisdom—but remember the boy in that bedroom, how overwhelmed yet entranced he was. Some days desolation has eaten me alive, feeling desolate around people, feeling not so much cut off as buried: too much hubbub around me, too many dramas, too many people putting me in their story and telling me they know me. The public world is a machine of hungry people who multiply everything. That everything wants to be more—"profits increased," to quote a daily mantra. You stand in a fast-food joint and look at the hamburgers jumping out one after another, and you feel you aren't any different from that hamburger.

People take photos of one another to still the desolation onslaught, but that's more multiplication. No photo can get the aloneness, that blank yet stolid feeling. Maybe the lonesomeness can be shown, though you would have to be a great artist to get the externals right. Aloneness is resistant, our last

fort. Sometimes when I've been in museums and seen por-
traits from hundreds of years ago, one person finally pictured,
I can feel that aloneness—this man or woman and no other.
I can feel how he or she sat in a chair and held the pose, how
that person and his or her thoughts are gone but the aloneness remains, the tension of a body in time and space, a boy
in a bed.

. . .

Shadow talking soft to the night—
That's where my road turns—
Couldn't catch the shape of the words—
They were and then they weren't.

"Not fair," kids yell at injustice, that self-assured mon-
ster, and kids are right, because over and over you are
put in the path of wrong that says it is right, how one kid in
the classroom is the teacher's pet and gets away with mischief
while another catches hell for existing, how one kid becomes
the class outcast, how one kid tries hard but no one cares.
Growing up is a long introduction to the faces of injustice.
You can shrug your shoulders and pretend you don't care. You
can fight back; though when you're a kid you're weak, so it's
more in your mind about what you would do if you could. Or
you can make it worse by piling on when someone is down, by
not sticking up for someone, by letting someone take the rap
for something you did, by acting above it all, or getting down
in the mud and slinging. You answer a taunt with another
taunt. You stand up for yourself and make yourself smaller.

There's a chorus in my head of all the certainty I've witnessed and read about—"That's the way it is and that's the way it should be"—that's turned out to be not so certain. Of course we hang people for stealing a crust of bread or don't let Negroes sit in the front of the bus or women vote. What of it? Prejudice already has decided the matter—shut up. One reason to make art is to oppose "of course."

The songs I wrote when I was young about race and warmongering and how poor people get the short end of the stick weren't political songs. They were injustice songs. I don't know if the songs accomplished anything. At some point you have to say, "Well, it's only a song." Have you helped to wake people up, or have you made them more complacent because they can agree with the song and feel smug? It can be hard to tell. A few of my injustice songs are almost anthems. Sometimes I've felt proud and sometimes I've felt uneasy. The iron wheels keep turning.

Messages make me nervous. Once you've said the obvious—or what to me felt obvious—then you can't go on saying it. Tedium sets in; self-righteousness sets in; conceit sets in. And you see how the finger-pointing and blaming never stop. What could honesty and power have to say to each other beyond "I'm right and you're wrong," or "I'm strong and you're irrelevant"? Almost humble, almost savvy, almost wary, I've tried to listen not lecture.

When you're young and you write about injustice, people say you've got your head in the clouds. When you get older and you say there's more to life than wrangling over the most capacious form of greed, people still say you don't know what you're talking about but—and it's one more put-down—that your musical head can afford to be in those clouds. But my head's been right on the ground, and what I hear, no matter what an election does or a public opinion poll says or a front page proclaims, are people's steps shuffling and lurching and falling down. The old news: Mortal fate is here to stay.

I've lost friends over politics—not because I disagreed but because I didn't show enough interest. When I tried to explain how organizations make me itch, they smiled or got impatient. Get real, they'd say. Most of them went to college and believed they had an earnest stake in how the public world ran. I'd ask them who decided what was important or exactly who was running the show or what happened to yesterday's papers, but they smiled that educated, keeping-up-with-current-events smile. My notion of events and theirs weren't the same. They were moving forward; I was caught. I heard time breathing hard—the seconds, days, and years accountable but elusive. I heard songs from tired voices that seemed to have no right to sing any song—women sitting by a child's bed late at night and men picking up a guitar after a day's labor. They did sing, though, soothing the universe inside themselves. I'd never say my notion was better. I've never trusted "better." People need to think they're standing on the last, highest hill. I'm not arguing, because I'd rather make up a song, but I'm not agreeing either.

* * *

Heard someone talking about bad news—
They said it wasn't bad—
Happened every day—could get worse—or just
Reasonably sad.

I wake in the middle of the night and don't know where I am
or who I am. I can feel my mind trying to find my body. In
those blurry seconds, I am the child who has been buried by
the years. I have no voice. I have no home. I have not so much
been abandoned as forgotten. I'm a gray face in the darkness.

Some reality speck kicks in: I'm on tour. This is the sev-
enth floor of a hotel in Sydney, Australia. Australia is the land
of kangaroos, though I've never seen a real one. All's well,
however—I've been located. Phantom Abe has been found, but
Abe is a phantom who will never be found. I don't exaggerate,
though I wish I could. We all live in our heads, but some of us
do it more than others. You can't see into the other heads, so
it's hard to tell. And just as well.

Once upon a time there would have been a woman beside
me in the king-size bed, a new acquaintance of the night
before, but that was a while ago. The time I'm thinking about
is the recent decade of my waking by myself and the feeling
that floods me. The feeling is unfocused: The hotel room's
details fade very quickly. I'm in another place—awake but not,
suspended in the firmament of imagination. My special atmosphere—I know it well. I'm headed nowhere and have nothing
to do but entertain my thoughts, memories, regrets, and fears.
At these dislocated moments, my privacy is sweetest. I tell

people about my dreams and have written songs about them, but this space of disconnected wakefulness is something else.

The sun is our daily joy, but imagination craves darkness. You read Poe's tales when you're thirteen and something in you goes, "Yes." In my hotel room I can close my eyes or keep my eyes open. It makes no difference. I'm inside of myself, the accumulated moments racketing around and calling for attention. If I weren't flattened on the bed on my back (how I sleep), I might nod my head. I see what's in the darkness—me. As I put it in a song: "There's no room service there / You best be more aware."

I'm abusing the first-person pronoun and acting as though there is more substance than there is. If you write about yourself, are you automatically excusing yourself? All I would seem to know is to play to an audience. Applause confirms me. I can afford to turn my back and say nothing. Still, I feel tissue-like, membranous. The darkness pours through me. I'm a sieve. What emerges then is some gist, an elongated moment, a splinter of feeling. I'm driving in a car somewhere in New Mexico. I'm with Patricia, whom I met through a friend and whose designs I've done nothing to resist. We don't have many clothes on, but we're young and don't need many clothes. We're both smoking cigarettes. She turns to me and tells me not to think she loves me. She wants me but doesn't love me. "Thanks," I say back. I can feel myself inhale and almost choke. She shakes her head and starts playing with a strand of her hair, which is auburn. Once I had asked her what color she called it, and she told me that word. She had laughed, a throaty but demure laugh, terrifically sexy. I could fall hard.

That's what I feel in the room: the highway wind rushing through the rolled-down windows and how hard I could fall. I'm suspended there in that car. She leans over and puts her tongue in my ear. She laughs again. I laugh too and I'm falling.

There's no story beyond that because there's no story in the first place. The moments can't be a story. That's why there are songs, because the moments can't be made into stories. Only songs can get at the moments, how spectacular they can be and how particular and how harrowing. I'm lying there in the king-size bed and I feel her tongue. Probably I'm not the only guy lying in a bed feeling a woman's tongue in his ear, but there's no woman next to me. It's time that I'm feeling.

I don't search for my guitar in the darkness. I don't turn on a light. I let the feeling sit with me. Something in me wants to moan. Something wants to dig back and stop time. I've written hundreds of endings to songs, but they all end the same way: That's the way it is, kid, get used to it—my dad's voice. You can say that more poetically. You can say it more graphically. But it comes down to the same sentiment, though not as bleak as you might think. It's better to feel than not to feel. And sometimes our wrong turns add up to a right turn. Start counting the feelings that begin with grade school when you look at someone and feel something sudden and strangely warm. No one told me about those feelings. What would they have said anyway? Enjoy it. Watch out.

"Eventually we parted" would be the story's predictable end, but that wouldn't be true. I can see her playing with her hair, and after another hour or so we pull over at a motel that's a mom-and-pop kind of place, people retired from up north who are making some income and don't mind living by the highway. It's late afternoon. We look a little disheveled, but the woman behind the counter is glad to see customers. She tells us where we can get supper—"just a few miles from here"—while Patricia smiles and stares down at the floor, as if she's shy. We make it to the room—number six out of eight rooms in a horizontal row—and explode onto one another. Or perhaps into one another is more like it—or both.

Go tell me what the ending to that is. Tell me how waking in the middle of the night is an invitation to the uncharted inland seas. The numbers on the nightstand's digital clock are another linear lie. Patricia's body, though, was the truth, the whinnies she made when I was inside her. I may be lost, but I can see in the dark, and hear too.

· · ·

Your face comes back but it's not you—
Your voice absorbs the light—
I thrash through sleep, through losing dreams
Then argue with the night.

Back when there were kings and queens, there were jesters and fools to hang out with them. The kings and queens were serious people who signed treaties and tore them up; the jesters and fools told jokes, juggled, made up riddles, did somersaults, and pulled off an occasional magic trick. Having a performer around made sense: You can only take so much seriousness, since most seriousness turns out to be one self-importance meeting another self-importance. What there is to be serious about—as in, does your love extend past your nose—doesn't usually fall into the serious category.

Some of my songs have been described as "goofy." I'm down with that; I like nonsense. Growing up and way past growing up, you listen to people telling you that they are making sense when they aren't. This can be very large, as in "We're going to go to war now. Make sense?" How much sense does starting a war make? Apparently a lot, since wars keep going on. Then afterward people notice the war may not have made so much sense. Maybe the enemies could have cooled their heels or gone for a walk or thought about how when you die you don't come back. Maybe we don't need more memorials.

If there were a jester around, he might tell the king before the war to take a look in the mirror and see who the fool was. I get it that the king might not like that, how he might tell the jester to get lost. I'm sure more than one jester was thrown down the well. Still, if there's no jester around, if everyone is serious all the time because that's what important people do—be serious—there's not much hope of wars stopping. Seriousness kills a lot more people than goofiness. I'd save seriousness for designing bridges.

And there's the feeling I've had forever that most of what got talked about was nonsense to begin with. I mean how one thing runs into another in our heads so we're talking about dogs and then grocery shopping and then something some senator said and then how a bunion hurts. Whoa! That's what I wanted to say when I was a kid. Whoa! What was that you said? It's okay to wander—that's what we do—but don't pretend it's more than it is. Speaking for my songs, the sense I make is elliptical and emotional: thoughts riding the surf of feelings. Every day we make verbal quilts then forget them.

So if I write that "Shap the King took a hefty swing at the broken ring of time," I'm letting a kind of nonsense make a kind of sense. I'm letting the words act out. I'm proposing my sense of making sense. That's what poetry does—serious goofing, unforeseen linking that captures the curves of our minds. I rhyme because rhyme mixes sense with nonsense best. In the traditions I inherited—ballads, songs, blues—rhyme was second nature. Rhyme has always seemed democratic to me—one person as good as another, one word connecting with another word, one moment greeting another, one image sparking another. It's the remarkable engine.

There's the chime of rhyme too, how little kids love how happy it feels in their mouths. My own kids were no exception. I'd hear them outside chanting their heads off—sometimes for the fun of it, sometimes making fun of one another, sometimes making stuff up—their own tall tales, their voices squealing with pleasure. BIG FAT CAT SAW BIG QUICK RAT! RUN! RUN! OOPS! YOU'RE DONE! I once asked my littlest girl, Esther, if she ever wrote down a rhyme. She looked at me as if I were crazy. "Daddy," she said, "I make them up."

From what I gather, poets turned against rhyme in modern times: too constricting, too trite, too common. But rhyme helps with the great question that poetry asks, that we never stop asking: What does one thing have to do with another? Rhyme is one way to find out, to let the mind navigate and see what it discovers, to indulge the wealth of sound. What I discovered when I started to get down to it, when I started writing songs that were mine and not nodding to someone else, was that rhyme could take me anywhere. Some critics called my lyrics surreal—a fancy word—but I don't agree. I just let rhyme take over and lead me. I trusted. I wasn't afraid or embarrassed. If things got weird or funny or intense, then things got weird or funny or intense—or all three at the same time.

I had a rhyming dictionary but threw it out. Rhyme couldn't be contained in a book. There were more words than I ever would use. I could push hard, or I could ease off so the sounds were barely there. I could tighten up so the rhymes were close together or loosen so the rhymes seemed to lope and almost get lost. I could elongate and shorten the syllables as I pleased. Typically I began with a tune, but the lyric wasn't far behind. You could feel the rhymes waiting there in the notes, impatient, full of bounce and jounce, uncrowned renown. I could go on. I have.

* * *

Quiet steps before the talk—
Murmurs like wind across
A lake that is more sea than lake—
One more thought gets lost.

Written sentences seem calm: There the words go, everything working toward being agreeably steady, the declarative pulse humming along, sure of its determining self. You surely wouldn't want to write one-word exclamations all the time. Yet what's paced in the pit of me, what gets the songs written, even the love songs, has been rage. How could that be? Interviewers would remark, "There's an edge of anger in your songs," while angling at something in my past or my politics or my lack of politics—my great, hidden grievance. I'd resist and evade, get bland: shucks and gee and well—another Regular Guy. "If you could look into my soul, you'd see it's vanilla," I'd spout agreeably. They'd nod, "but . . ." We'd go a few rounds to no conclusion.

Anger and rage are different. Someone does something to you and you get angry. Rage is more like a condition, a kind of internal burning. When I started to read Shakespeare's tragedies, I recognized rage: Those kings were impossible people filled with impossible ambition. They were born entangled— other kings and princes opposing them. The only way out for them was through rage. The rage in them was about frailty, how their power only went so far, how the crown could fall and crack, how they who seemed to be everything weren't, how they were merely human.

I wasn't a king and didn't live in a play, but I had my rage. I felt, as if it were an insult, the plain idiocy of every day's news, the spectacle of wrong insisting it's right, the public grief we get to share. And we're born into hard, personal facts that have nothing to do with the sweetness of taking a breath—my dad thinking about his brother, my mom wishing her quiet wishes. We're born into a web of circumstances called "time." We take the web for granted: None of us is surprised to be born. Here are your parents. Here is the hospital. Here is the house you will live in. The street has a name. You have a name. We cry for sustenance and gradually adapt. We learn to keep our crying to ourselves.

I was sarcastic and touchy. "What do you know, man?" might have been written under my photo in the high school yearbook. You could say I was conceited, the way a teacher would say, "Who do you think you are, Abraham Starker? The rules apply to you too." I wasn't out to make trouble, but there was a gap between what was announced and what happened. I didn't want to live in that gap, where the chief occupation was the unhappiness of what people thought they deserved and what they got. You could hear it in people's voices, how the men tried to make up for it with heartiness and the women with cooing. Neither convinced me. The dreaminess of love never worked because you couldn't live in a dream. The feeling that you were bound to be some kind of hero never worked because the world wasn't interested in heroes. "Just do your job," my dad would say. Did he mean to console or confine me?

In our town there was a Civil War statue of a Union soldier that I used to look at. I thought about those soldiers, some of whom were my age, as much boys as men. They joined up, they fought, and they died. I would have done the same thing. The reality made me queasy—how my own skin was not just per- ishable, which I first understood when I fell down the stairs at age three, but how I was one more in a very long line. All my precious thoughts were worthless. Time used me as much as I used time. No matter what I did, I was doing as I was told.

I fumed, advancing one ardent step forward and retreat- ing one cynical step back. No one cared. I was Abe the truck company owner's son—not much going on with that iden- tity. Another guy trying to attract the chicks by playing in a band and copping an attitude. Let the kid rave. What could he understand? What could he do? Where could he go? He didn't even own a car.

"Rave on," as the great Buddy Holly put it, "rave" being close to "rage." There was a good time in rage, letting my passion out in songs and not caring what anyone thought. If I hadn't done that, my feelings would have strangled me. Later, when I had the chance, I could be cruel: putting people down while smiling a nasty smile, a hipster behind his sunglasses, the rage mentholated. Those were defenses, but they were threats too. Abe, the metaphysical gangster, already had been crossed: too much time and too much space, too little time and too little space. No one, short of God, was going to do that again to him. And as for God . . .

Someone once showed me a poem by the poet Rilke about a panther. In the poem the panther is caged and weary of going back and forth in that miserable prison with its "thousands of bars." Back in the 1950s and 1960s, people who tried to think twice talked about the cage as "the system" and how hard it was to do anything about "the system." I never doubted that there were some conniving hands at the big wheel, but I didn't subscribe to the struggle against what I couldn't see. For me the struggle has been personal. Artists are bound to take their art that way. When the world made a fuss about my songs, I was pleased but surprised. They were my songs that arose out of my circumstances. It turned out, though, that they weren't. It's what you'd call curious, how that works—how mine can be yours, how we share the rage, even if we don't call it that, even if we barely recognize it.

. . .

Fire inside burns a person up—
Turns a soul to ash—
Leaves a voice gone but free—
The life—A hardened flash.

The poems they had us read in school didn't feel like part
of life. They stood on a pedestal—all perfect and important—and we were supposed to walk around them and not
touch but talk in hushes. They made me feel stupid. Could
I understand them? Was I good enough or smart enough or
sensitive enough? And what were these poems in textbooks
for? They seemed like they got written to be in textbooks, all
formal and high-tone yet airless and sunless. What was the
real occasion for them? There must have been one, but I don't
recall any teacher telling us. We had to find out what they
meant; our job began and ended there. Once we figured that
out, the poem was done, as if it were a tire and we took the air
out.

Poetry seemed to exist on a cloud somewhere far away
from where I lived. When our tenth-grade English teacher,
Mrs. Holzer, read from *Idylls of the King* or *Evangeline* (actually,
she used to say, "Now I will declaim, class"), Bill Saint Pierre,
who sat behind me and who'd drop out of school the next
year to work in his father's garage, used to whisper, "They're
punishing us. What did we do to be punished?" Poetry was a
reason to raise your hand to go to the bathroom and hide out
until the teacher remembered you were gone and sent someone to fetch you. We all sat there trying to stay awake, though

some of the girls pretended they liked it. Maybe they did. Girls could act in unaccountable ways.

I knew there was supposed to be something special about poetry, not from school but from remarks people would make about something being "poetry" or someone remembering some lines from a poem and reciting them. I can't say either of those things happened often, but when they did, I remembered. Anything out of the ordinary I remembered, and poetry was out of the ordinary. That seemed to be the point of poetry, but what we heard and read in school tended to be a bad kind of out-of-the-ordinary, like getting sick at dinner and having to go up to your room. It felt strained.

The words, though, attracted me as words. They seemed to be bobbing or marching or thumping along (a lot of them felt like thumping), but they were active, and they each had a strength. They mattered; although, at the same time, they seemed cramped because of the poems they were in. The words couldn't breathe. When the teacher said we were going to study a poem, I felt this categorical strangeness, as if she were going to take a piece of uranium out of her desk.

I wondered what it would be like to free the words, to go to places beyond the poems we were shown. I had a sense that there could be a force to words, but the force didn't have to act special. The force was there in the drama of what people did to one another. Even in something as predictable as school, there would be moments when things got tense between two kids or a kid and a teacher. You could feel how a word could be explosive, how when someone said, "That's not true," or "Take it back," there was this edge inside of words waiting to come out.

The dramas in my head needed the words, and the words needed the dramas. I needed a stage. Getting up and playing the guitar was one stage, but the words were another. I liked the songs about finding love and losing love, but I figured out pretty quickly there was more going on than the sighs of romance. What about all those feelings I had about how I didn't fit in and had to leave where I grew up and the whole mess of needles and pins that seemed to be there every day? "Live with it," my dad would say about my complaints, but what I felt were more than complaints. There were the quiet torments that went with living, the feeling that you're going the wrong way but don't know how to change. And there were torments out there that weren't quiet, torments that ended with screams and even guns. There were mysteries too, the in-between of shaking your bewildered head, unknowns that words might pierce.

No one cared much about words. We did grammar drills and wrote "themes," as they used to call them. We took vocabulary tests, words that we were supposed to know; though I couldn't imagine telling someone something was "meretricious." Looking in the dictionary was a chore, like trying to find something in the medicine cabinet. Words, though, were one thing that no one could take away. If they came out of my mouth, then they were mine. If they came out of my pen, they were even more mine. I could be known by my words, a thought, whether vain or not, that pleased me. I could use words not to make things go away but to make them be more there.

What I found my way into was the life of words, which was what I was looking for in poetry. A few times in school, I felt that when I was reading Robert Frost. Though the process felt embalmed, as in "what does line five mean," there was something in there pulsating. He was a little too sure of himself for my taste. I couldn't imagine the pieces inside me fitting together the way the pieces inside him seemed to fit. Still, I could imagine talking to him and listening to him (probably more listening than talking) in a way I couldn't imagine with other poets we read.

He probably would have had his problems with me. That I was Jewish and from some small town in the Midwest would have been too freaky. How could someone like me be a poet? There was nothing poetic about a life of "Pass the meatloaf," or "It's going to rain tomorrow." Life ground the words down to dust. The craziness in life, though, was there for the taking. My feeling was to let the words be crazy—focused but crazy. The words in a Tin Pan Alley song were agreeable—that was the whole notion behind the song—but I wanted the words to do more than pass the time in a lilting way. I wanted words you could hiss and spit, words that could darken like the sky before a summer storm. If that was disagreeable, too bad.

· · ·

Emily D came by to shoot
The usual poetic breeze—
"Infinity" gives me hives—
"Eternity" makes me sneeze.

When people asked me why I left college, as if everything had to have a reason, I answered with my best crooked smile that college was too many reasons in a small space, that everything felt too smooth, too logical, too laid out, too self-assured. Sitting and listening to the professors lecture, as if they were in some sort of mental compartment on a mental train going to the destination of their choice, was weirdly strenuous—so much exertion. Around me everyone was taking notes and looking the serious-student part: This is how you become an adult. I could have passed out from boredom. After you have a reason, what then? Do we rise on a reasonable cloud to some precise heaven? Don't we all come from the dirt of feeling?

"Dropout" is not a happy word. Neither of my parents was pleased. You can't blame them. I wasn't doing what I was supposed to be doing. The Jews are people of the book not the guitar. My mom told me I was "headstrong." I probably was more heart-strong, but I understood her. I was throwing over what seemed like my chance to live an orderly and fulfilling life for the opportunity to do something that probably wasn't an opportunity at all—singing for spare change and hanging out with other people singing for spare change. Scuffling.

I couldn't stay in school, though. I was too restless. Maybe once upon a time I was the Wandering Jew. Maybe I was the shadow you don't see when you look over your shoulder. I couldn't take "yes" for an answer and I couldn't take "no" because I resented answers. I tried to make sense to my parents when I came home and told them I'd had it, but I could feel, even as I said the words, that I didn't make much sense. If you don't do what you're supposed to do, then you aren't making sense. They told me I was spoiled. I had a chance to make something of myself, a chance I was throwing away. Only spoiled people did that—or people shot into the unknown from the cannon of possibility.

Their words stung, but I couldn't be someone I wasn't. I told them not to worry, things would turn out okay, but they knew I was putting a good face on what was not much more than willfulness. I remember sitting at the dining room table on a Saturday morning and my parents drinking instant coffee and eating these crullers they liked and me trying to make the best of things by at least being polite, by nodding my needs-a-haircut head and listening. My mom cried some. I left that afternoon, which meant a guy I knew was headed to Chicago. From there I'd go somewhere, which meant New York City.

For most people I wound up playing with in Chicago and then New York, the music making and the song making were a time of life, something they did for a while and then moved on. You couldn't make a living, for starters. You were dependent on clubs that had problems paying the rent, much less the performers. There were too many acoustic guitars and not enough stages for an audience that was never that big to begin with. America was busy moving to the suburbs and watching television, not going to hear someone sing "Midnight Special" or "Pretty Polly" or some original, poem-like song. I had started to write such songs.

None of that bothered me. It should have, but all that mattered was my liberation. Whatever I did, I had to get free from what other people thought I should be. Playing my guitar (a band seemed way more than I could handle, and rock 'n' roll was going through one of its droughts) and making up songs was a loose category of low expectations. Probably some of my parents' friends told them not to fret, that I was just going through a "stage." Unfortunately, I'd been at that stage since I was five years old. I'd reached the age where I could follow my legs out the door. I could put my unease in a duffel and head east.

The blues guys down South had a genuine cause for their unease—a black man was a marked man. I didn't pretend to be black, but I felt like a marked man because I felt how made up everything is, how none of what everyone took for granted had to be that way. The pin the world danced on was imagination, but the world took it for a fact. Hard as that was to explicate, I was bound to live in that no-place where imagination challenged every move. There were times down the road when I was smoking a joint with other guitar pickers and hangers-on that I tried to make that no-place credible. "You live where, Abe?" someone would ask. "Between Reality and Unreality? Is that your postal address? Existentialville?" We'd all laugh with the good nature that came from smoke. I'd wink or pull a dismayed face as if I were only fooling, take another hit, and let time keep elongating.

I suspect much art comes from uneasiness. I've made up songs not to hide my unease but to expose it. "I don't know and you don't know. Why can't we admit it?" If I've lived a movable life, on the road for most of the year, it's because I'd mind-rot if I sat still—the way I'd have mind-rotted had I stayed in that wooden seat back in college. A person has to listen to those promptings. You may get nothing more back than the ill taste of your delusions, but it's your taste, not someone else's.

. . .

Carved my initials on a desk—
Stared at the back of a head—
Save me from knowing, I told the air—
Let me live undead.

One day during my brief college tenure, I was in a guy's room down the dormitory hall; he had told me I could look through his collection of poetry books, an offer no one had ever made me. He went off to class and I stayed there, looking at this paperback and that hardbound and then picking up a book of someone named William Blake, not a name I knew from anywhere. He wasn't in any of the textbooks they gave us in high school, or, if he was, I was asleep the day he popped up for the next test.

I sat on a hard wooden chair, the only chair in the room, and started reading something called *Songs of Innocence and Experience*. When the guy came back from his class, I was still sitting there. I remember looking up and wondering who this person was who had just come through the door and what room I was in. A very big mind had enveloped me. I sat there in a Blake cloud, and I must have said something like "William Blake." I can't imagine I could have done anything like finish a sentence. The guy—I'm thinking his name was Joe—said something like "cool" and indicated he'd appreciate it if I left so he could go on with his life. "Mind if I borrow this?" I asked. He was gracious: "Blake's the man. Keep digging it." End of formative moment. Beginning of the Brotherhood of the Wandering Poets Society. Shot of stunned Abe shambling down the hallway to his room, oblivious, but brimming with intuitions.

Reading Blake that day was like watching the seed of life split open: Here it is, what you couldn't say that somehow must be said. Nothing ever was going to be the same; the way it was when I first heard Robert Johnson or Woody Guthrie or Buddy Holly, nothing was going to be the same. I thought back to my high school textbook, which had some name like *Adventures in Literature*. Adventures! Their adventures and mine were different.

Once I started reading him, I understood why William Blake wasn't the main course. He didn't belong with the people in charge. The newspapers threw around the word "rebellious," but that was only a word to pick on young people who weren't doing what they had been told to do. Blake was more than a rebel. In his proverbs and songs, he was reordering the whole path of our perceptions, beginning with good and bad. He was looking for a deeper root than one person feeling superior to another person because of money or family or race or religion. England had its lords, but no one could lord over William Blake.

"A good apple tree or a bad is an apple tree still: A horse is not more a lion for being a bad horse, that is its character." Blake wasn't tossing out the words "good" and "bad." He wasn't one of those people who said, "Well, that's just your judgment, Abe," as if people didn't make dozens of judgments every day, as if making judgments wasn't a basic part of being human, as if I was supposed to be some objective robot. Blake was standing up for the character of creatures, the way they were in their being. What a relief that was, to hear someone say that, for letting it be, for not straining.

"Excessive sorrow laughs. Excessive joy weeps." That was the well of feeling I wanted to jump into. That was the well, however deep and dark, inside of me. When you have that well of feeling, it can turn around on you. It can batter you. So I smoked cigarettes. So I made jokes about my awkwardness and told tall tales about myself. So I stood up and played my songs. Although I was performing, I was insisting on myself as a person. That seemed the peculiar American essence I was searching for, which sounds like no big thing but was. Somehow, it seemed that no songwriter had done that before. The song came before the person. You could recognize a song by Cole Porter or Woody Guthrie or Robert Johnson, but the kind of song came first. There was no kind-of-song for me. It was as if I was the song.

Once I'd found out who Blake was and that such a person had lived, I felt I had a companion. He was impenitent. He was glad with delight. He obliterated goodness. When people criticized me for not going to bat for the latest cause, I wanted to point to Blake and how he understood that too often goodness was one more thought conspiracy. Go into where people are—not where they should be—and try to find out about that. Go where the words seem to end but don't. Go where your head opens. The beauty of his poems was that his words weren't soft or fuzzy with well-meaning; they were hard and true as stone.

. . .

Joy scouts knocked on my front door
Checking out high times—
Bamboozled swoon—here and now!
Lust-struck?—step inside.

Since I split from college, I became someone who taught himself, an autodidact. My reading was more gaps than wholes, but words may have struck me more because of that. Whatever terrain I was crossing was mine, not a course syllabus. The maps I made were my own. Along the way people turned me onto this writer and that one. There were used bookstores in Chicago and New York where you could sit and no one would bother you. The owners were happy to talk books. I read Balzac, all that frenzy about money and envy. I read about Indian chiefs, some truly noble men. I read about slavery and mines and immigration and FDR and fiction by Faulkner and Thomas Wolfe and Willa Cather. And one by one I learned about the poets, the real ones who were bigger than a textbook, the ones who threw the textbooks away. That would have been Blake, Rimbaud, Walt Whitman, the haunting Emily Dickinson (who taught me a thing or two about quatrains), and Coleridge with his "Kubla Khan" and Shelley, what gets called "Romantic," which seemed off the mark, as if you had to be categorized if you let out too much feeling in too different ways, as if that wasn't what poets were supposed to be doing all along.

Those poets had a hard time staying in their skin. I could feel that reading their poems. They were in trances. Their words weren't so much knocking on the door of feeling as knocking the door down. "Through sensitivity / I wasted my life," wrote Rimbaud. He had no interest in gushing over flowers. Nothing against the flowers. Things just got too neat, too in a row. Things got too simple, too how-you-were-supposed-to-respond. You had to be able to turn against yourself as much as go with yourself.

I read that when Blake looked at the sun, he said he saw a host of angels. Poets have visions, and the visions are as true as the so-called reality—really truer, because the great poets see into things rather than the surface. They glimpse the energy that dwarfs us, though their glimpses can't help but be unsettling. Those glimpses, which is what poems are, ruin the daily certainty of purposes, but they also put more air in your lungs, passion in your blood, and fire in your head. They inspire you about being here, how deep everything runs, the millennia that charge every moment. And if you do what they do, if you traffic in words, they give you something to aim for and something to live in. I didn't aspire to lose my life the way some poets did. I did aspire to honor whatever vision I had.

Though the guys I've been around who sell and market my records will talk about "vision," they mean something else. They mean they can slot imagination and make it comfortable. "You can get this." "This is right for you." "You'll be in with the in-crowd, or out with the out-crowd." Whether it's Buicks or records, commerce reduces matters to a size that fits into a very small pocket.

The vision I'm talking about doesn't fit. The vision I'm talking about makes its own space. It can happen like

Shakespeare's playhouse happened (another subject I read about), though poets back then had their problems—no money, booze, sex, bad tempers. Being in Christopher Marlowe's skin couldn't have been easy. The visions can add to the uneasiness that drove you to the vision in the first place. Meanwhile, you're smiling as much as you can smile—why not? Or you're not smiling, but the world, or certainly America, expects you to smile because that's what we do to reassure one another, along with the uplift provided by battalions of therapists, counselors, aides, analysts, advisers, consultants, coaches. As a kid, you grasp the distraction that too often surrounds the smiles, but after a while you go along because you want to get along. Your skin toughens. You get to be grown up. What atomic bomb?

Not everyone manages, however, and that's where my songs have gone—for those who don't quite manage or who manage badly or who don't understand what there is to manage or who don't want to manage in the first place, who are willing to admit how fractured the whole is. It's not like I've been able to put the pieces back together, but each song is a clue to the brokenness. To me that's comforting, like reading a Dickinson poem that's all tilted, but you're able to walk better after you read it because you stop bugging yourself about your own tilt.

As much as anything, the poets are alarms. The human pulse that poems insist on beats as it beats. Can you hear it? Can you hear the alarm that rings for every feeling that is pushed aside—rage and joy both interfering with business as usual? If I've protested anything, it's the pushing aside. In a country where business rules, the pushing goes without saying. Emotions aren't efficient or profitable. Songs really can go for a song, which the music publishers showed when they paid the artist who wrote it chump change for the rights. It happened to me at the beginning.

People came to America because they wanted to leave a life behind them or they were forcibly moved here, which makes for generations of ghosts, their aims born of hard hearts and hopeful hearts, each person looking forward to something the old language couldn't say. Each person trying to endure in a strange land that is bound to remain strange while insisting it isn't strange at all. "That Runyan guy is strange." I heard that plenty. They were right.

. . .

Lulu told me to blow this town—
Henry said, "Get real"—
No leaves on the tree outside my house—
No feelings left to feel.

My improbable task (which no one asked me to take on) has been to fill the emptiness peculiar to America. Growing up, I felt how out of proportion everything was, how the land was so much bigger than the people, what slim assertions the houses and stores were. Maybe it's that way everywhere, but often when I'm falling asleep, what I see is the highway heading out of my town and into the impenetrable darkness of night and sky and the silence of what seemed like endless land. How pitiful that road was, yet how important. One day I left on that very road.

Who knows how many times I've driven across the country? I've been in every state. I've looked out the window at the scenery, felt the wind on my face, turned the radio up. America seems more about going from one place to another than staying in one place. From the beginning it's been that way, the restlessness of purpose and the beckoning of elsewhere, the not-quite-knowing-what-to-do-with-yourself but being excited anyway. I'd be driving with a buddy or a lover headed to one of the coasts but willing to take a detour, never in too big of a hurry. I liked to pull into some town and go to a local place and have dinner, some place where even after I became famous people barely looked up, and if they did I just said, "No, but people have said I look like him." Then I liked to walk around and feel all those lives in all those houses. I can't know them and wouldn't want to, but I could imagine the sense of each person—brooding, forgetting, laughing, and a thousand other dramas—in those houses. I was in one once.

I get to be the perpetual stranger. It's not a prize everyone wants. My way of belonging is through my songs, which is the long way around the barn. "You could have stayed here and made a life like your sister did," my parents reminded me. They knew I couldn't have, but that didn't stop them. We fill the emptiness by having established lives—doing whatever work we do and living with our partner and our kids or living without a partner but still raising kids or living with other people in a house or just living alone. The variations seem to keep growing. People who drift—and I've been called, among many other things, "a spiritual wanderer"—don't reach the establishment stage. They remain porous, walking around at night and drinking in the emptiness, a big draft of nothing, going back to their hotel room and writing a song.

The songs show me there's more there than I thought was there. There's more feeling and more particularity and more scenes and more dramas. That's reassuring and has kept me in my skin I'd otherwise be jumping out of. When you drift, you can feel awfully arbitrary. People may know your name and people may want favors from you, but you can feel how off-center you are, how you've willed your life as much as you've lived it, how you keep heading toward something that isn't there. Maybe all that makes me American.

Part of the stranger role is being Jewish on both sides of my family, a few thousand years of being on the outside and looking in. It seems natural that I've wanted to take on the characters and situations I've made up in my songs. I'm making up for lost time. I'm making up for what was denied to my forebears. And I'm staking a claim—me too, mine too. There's a special reverberation to the emptiness for me. My people kept to themselves and were kept to themselves. I remember when I first came upon the word "ghetto" and looked it up. What was that about? How could we be that wicked? How did we live? Barely and deeply, I came to realize.

"Don't fence me in" is an American sentiment. If you come from people who have been fenced in, you might want out. You might want to try to belong to the bigger world and see what that's like. You might lose yourself there, a worry that was my mom's about me before she died, how making good has been a form of losing myself. I told her the truth, though, how the Jewish part of me never goes away. How could I lose something that ingrained? Every time I speak, I hear it in my intonation, that sort of bemused whine. Wheedling Abe, peddling mercies and insights. I don't think of that as a bad thing. It comes with my terrain: trying to figure things out while making things up. Those things could get nasty. I've read the history: Things have gotten very nasty.

Not here in America, my dad would remind me, as he sat there in his Barcalounger fastness, but I'd remind him about the slavery ships and piles of buffalo skulls and the people chewed up in factories. How much nastiness comes with the price of admission? Signs saying "No admittance"; fences saying "Stay out"; schools saying "Don't apply"—a long list of signs. Enough forbidding amid the constant cheerleading to turn a life bitter.

Since there's no container that holds the emptiness, you can't fill it in. It's formless. What fills that formlessness is energy, an energy I've been as drunk on as anyone. All that driving here and there has been drunken. You see everyone behind the wheel, sometimes looking serious and thinking about where they're going and what's supposed to happen next and sometimes singing along to some music; but the driving is a species of intoxication that comes with notions of purpose and purposelessness, of urgency and just driving around, notions that have nothing to do with alcohol. American songs vibrate with that driven energy, which is why a fair portion of the world fell in love with rhythm and blues and then rock 'n' roll. That energy is how my songs got written. What they point to is beyond me: There's no sorting out the energy or the emptiness. What we do in the United States is use the land—that sense of vastness—to fuel our imaginations.

I've never asked what the land wants from me. I'm as guilty as anyone, another blind, excitable blip. That's one more thing I think about in the middle of the night, how easy it is to take from the earth, how pale my excitement is beside the patience of the mountains and rivers, how pale, and how the bill is going to come due.

∘ ∘ ∘

Lived in a sod house where the light was dark—
Watched the tornado coming—
Huddled to keep the sky away—
Heard that hard wind humming.

I was in study hall trying to solve a trigonometry problem. I wasn't very good at trig. It always seemed as though there was something there that I couldn't see, and that frustrated me, as if I were trying to look around a corner with a head and neck that weren't made to look around corners. I didn't notice that Mary was standing there in front of me. She made a little "ahem" sound to get my attention. "Abe," she said, "we're not going together anymore." She paused to finger a necklace she was wearing, a thin chain of glass beads. "I'm afraid what they say about Jews is true." She turned and walked out of the room.

I looked down at the lined piece of paper I was working on. Cosines danced before my distracted eyes. The pencil in my hand felt heavy. What was I doing holding a pencil? What was I doing sitting in this room with its blackboards and one-piece wooden chair-desks on which a modest galaxy of initials had been carved? Mary, with whom I had been going for a couple of months and with whom I had exchanged caresses and kisses and fumbling intimacies that stopped well short of going all the way but still got us very excited, had said something to me that exploded my head on a couple of counts. She was out of my life, and it had something to do with my being Jewish. I put down my pencil very carefully as if it too might explode.

I felt as though something inside of me had been torn out and displayed to me, except that I didn't know what it was. I felt betrayed—a dark, metallic taste. I didn't know what to say, even to myself. Something telling had happened in a place where nothing more telling happened than people yawning or trying to do their homework. Something had happened that shouldn't have happened to me, maybe to someone in a book or movie, but not to me in my more-or-less sleepy little town. I hadn't deserved this.

Or had I? There was no one to talk the matter over with. I wasn't going to beg or thunder. I knew Mary was probably standing with some of her girlfriends and they were nodding their heads and probably grinning or saying that I got what I deserved. I looked at my desk-chair and it seemed askew, as if the floor had shifted. The taste in my mouth felt worse, not better. My stomach started to churn the way it did the time I shared a fifth of whiskey with my buddy Jimmy Pappas. I staggered to the boys room and threw up.

I'm not sure my head has ever cleared up from that moment. I can't say I became one of those Jews who's always on guard. No one ever said anything like that to me again. Most Americans

I've met never cared what I was or where I came from. America was a big stew, and I was another ingredient. I was bound to be changed. No one stayed pristine. And I was bound to be hard to identify, the old where-did-you-say-you-come-from and you-know-I-have-a-cousin-who-lives-out-there.

Mary did identify me. Her words left me feeling that for me to stay who I was, I needed to become someone else. I needed to join America in my way. What so many Americans took for granted—that they belonged here—was not going to work for me. You wouldn't say what Mary said if I were another Christian American. Would she have walked up to Tim Anderson, who sat next to me in trig, and said, "You're such a Swede." I don't think so. The invisible mark was on me, the one that went back forever, the one I had ignored because who cared about such an old story that took place in a desert?

It kept taking place, though, and that became part of my situation, how nothing died, least of all history. Whether the history was about Jews or a woman who burnt a cache of love letters or an Indian who left the reservation and never returned or any of what I've made into songs was immaterial. You could focus on what people thought you were, or you could elude those thoughts by making up your own. I wasn't going to hide, but I wasn't going to believe what Mary or anyone told me about myself. Her head was full of uselessness. Too many heads turned out to be like that, but that wasn't my affair. My affair was to learn about betrayal, about that taste in my mouth and how it never went away.

It took some determination, some talking to the mirror in my bedroom, but the next time I saw Mary in the hall in school, I didn't look away. I gave her a level look. She acted as if I wasn't there. If someone is just an idea in your head, then I wasn't there. But I knew I was. And I felt something like happy.

. . .

> I brought my clock and vacant frown—
> I brought my papers and black silk coat—
> Not enough, the padrone snarled and snapped—
> You can't board the immigrant boat.

One word for song is "ditty," a tuneful, little musical event that celebrates some incident or mood. Ditties pass the time agreeably, especially when time gets long and heavy. I've written some. Foolery, as I've noted, is close to my heart. Many of my songs, though, are nothing like ditties. The images dance and beckon and sometimes almost glitter, but the songs present far-reaching failures, largely my own.

Everyone writes about falling in love, but falling out of love has called my name just as often. One woman told me it was a "dis-ease" I had, one that went with my twin, unease. I didn't argue. There's the falling in love, the lust and romance tangle, but before that there's the love in my mind, which seems always too large and too strong and too much for the woman standing in front of me, who remains one modest human being brushing her hair or doing her nails. Before I move toward her, I'm skewered by desire that insists on what can be or should be or wants to be. There's no movie starlet image, but that may make it worse, the rapt vagueness of my feeling, like a swooning before anything happens so I'm not present when things do happen. I've gone someplace else, where words rush in, where one mistake greets another.

Dozens and dozens of songs about women, as if they were a continent I'd been trying to explore but somehow kept getting lost like Columbus and then saying I was found. Or looking for the feeling of being completed, not my other half but my other whole. Something about the unsettling reality of men and women, their differences, and how we pass over that but never really pass over that because how could we? We're always simmering. The tension comes and goes, the attraction does too. I've been a prisoner, but I've liked being a prisoner. I've liked the endless tug and the disillusion that's my own doing.

"You'll never tell the truth," another woman said to me. "That's why you write all these songs." Women know, don't they? I guess if you've spent however many thousands of years watching men blunder around, you've built up some smarts. The thing is that I want to tell truths; that's one place the songs come from and what makes them more than ditties. Disillusion is a major truth, yet if you feel that you're bound to go down that path, that's wrongheaded. That's more like some inner bleakness that won't go away, bleakness even when it's valentines and laughter and bodies enjoying each other.

My rap sheet says three divorces and a couple of long-term relationships. That tells you something, but numbers don't do the pain justice. What's left, long after the sweet years have evaporated, is this feeling that on the bad nights makes me wonder what's the point of being such a definitively clueless human being. Yet why should I pretend to be any wiser about matters of the blood than anyone else? I've never settled, but the women haven't either. All three of the marriages told me they got tired of being my wife, of being a Mrs. That wasn't who they were; they weren't interested in pretending. Then there was life on the road and women offering themselves. As a guy in one of my bands once put it, "Abe, I'm not doing this because I like your songs or the money. I like the women."

The songs circle back to the situation and the complications and the moods and points of view—hers and his. The songs circle back to how there is no going back, how the finality of she's-gone is ever present, how one moment can set the other moments on fire and nothing is left, not even ashes. Some of the situations, of the guy-wakes-up-one-morning-and-his-woman-says-we're-done-get-out-of-here variety, are closer to horror than some masked phantom waving a knife. But that's the reality staring at you, how there's this churning going on, adjustment and readjustment and then a rupture, a tearing. "I can't do this anymore." Hard words to say and hard words to hear.

The key force on earth is what happens between men and women, the male and female, Adam and Eve, yin and yang. I don't just mean sex. I mean the electric web of understanding and misunderstanding, attraction and repulsion, longing and satiation. I mean the sticky confusion that's led me forward and taught me nothing and everything. Do I exaggerate? Not at all; the challenge is to say enough or something like enough, which I'll never do. Every woman is a door into another, a different place from the one I know. Every woman is telling me something. "And does that mean, Abe, you have to put your greedy hands on each one of them?" which kicks me back once more to yes and no. My urges have been impractical but not wholly carnal. If you want to find out more about what's missing in you, there's nothing wrong with asking questions. Being with women is first of all a question about what's missing in me.

"But that's not love," the voices say. But who is to say and decide that? As my Grandma Reva, who had her own problems in the love department, used to put it, "Sometimes you should look before you leap." Fair advice, but what's driven me with women is, despite all my songs, unknown. If love is about resting and accepting and saying, "Well, that's that," then it's not love. If love is a testing, then it's love. If the testing leads to one breakdown or another, it's no less love. Love has failure built into it. It's not just that one person can't encompass another or love the other person equally but that the other sex is a place you can never reach for all your trying. For all the heart misery, my head in my erring hands, that's been a cockeyed blessing.

* * *

Hard letter came the other day—
"Are you here anymore?"—
I am but what's inside can't see—
Knocks on a ruined door.

Reva used to talk about the old country, back in Russia where there were peasants and mud, dark bread and the czar's soldiers. She would go into a kind of singsong lament about the Jews and how hard they had it, how America was the end of their bondage. She wasn't, by any stretch, what you could call a patriot. American ways were permanently peculiar to her. Sometimes when one of my dad's truckers would show up at the house, usually a big, raw-boned guy, she would look him over as if he was going to pull out a knout or whip at any moment. As if a pogrom were lurking, she never stopped looking around furtively. When she heard secondhand about some people from Minneapolis who were going to visit the village in Ukraine where their people came from, she shook her head and made a sound of disgust. You couldn't have paid her to go back.

I've never visited the old country, but I've imagined myself being at home there. That's more about the slowness of life, conserving what might be precious, how hurry is never the way to go. Making music is about taking it slow and easy. Even when you're rocking, when you're burning, it's still note by note. You have to take the time to play the notes. The notes don't care about progress or the future or tomorrow. The notes don't care if we explore space or invent a bigger bomb. The notes come from a very old country—sounds from instruments. Once I heard someone playing the jawbone of an ass, the teeth jangling, and I thought I was hearing a voice from the pit of time, when people first began to listen to the sounds they could make.

It's the old news that interests me. That's been hard to explain, why I would want to be out of it. Modern times are about being with it. I'm not indifferent to what's going on—I keep listening to younger players—but I've heard enough buzz, especially that someone is the next me. And here I thought each one of us was singular! What the buzz says is that everything can be touted as singular because it's new but really is generic, because if it were too singular, people would get frightened. "Stay in the center of the lane but act as though you're interested in the edges" was how my first manager put it. I fired him.

What's kept speaking to me in the old ballads is their unswerving feeling—the testimony of blind passions and hovering darkness. There's a knife's edge in those songs: lost love, abandonment, sudden death, revenge, stolen kisses, rivalries, the feeling that we're held in the tangle of our memorable circumstances, some of our own making and some not. The ballads gave me a pleasure that was historical, the feeling of drama as both located and timeless, but also something else, the feeling that people lived a step or two away from every kind of duress—what once got called "fate"—and that it would be a mistake to push that insight aside. We may have cars and electricity, but we still live in the ballad world. Inventions create new ways, but every fatal crash points to those sad refrains.

Much excitement has passed me by. I would get requests from reporters asking if I had an opinion about this or that—a political controversy, a movie, some band making a big splash. If I said that such matters didn't concern me, I'd sound stuck up. I wasn't, but I wasn't interested in giving an opinion about something I didn't care about. What I cared about was how I was part of the old news, the perennial papers, what we might conserve.

If you grew up the way I did, a certain sense of belonging was denied you on account of your being Jewish, on account of your living far away from the hubbub of the cities, on account of your family barely having a history in America. In school I studied the Pilgrim-white-wooden-church story, but what could such people mean to me? What I came to learn was that incitements lurked within an endless array of American figures—outlaws, musicians, hustlers, politicians, ball players, actresses, pioneers, firebrands, even preachers. As a boy I wanted to be Davy Crockett or Daniel Boone, the primitive but righteous American as portrayed by Disney. As an adult I wanted to make a self of many selves so I could experience some of the everything there was to experience. In my songs I could be with a woman trapped on a volcanic island or a refugee at the city gates or a Civil War soldier gone west to prospect or a rich girl in New York City who finds she isn't rich anymore: the lost but sometimes the found.

Such travails and occasional joys were what my grandma called "the round of life." According to her, the old country was the round of life: seasons and customs and duties, one after another in their appointed order. There was some order in America—traffic lights and elections—but not much. I had a chance to enter into the life of the country and make my own order. How did I know that? I wish I knew. Or I don't wish. It's best if the impulse remains opaque. I see myself noodling around with my first guitar. Could I feel this was the ticket to something more than a kid in his bedroom? Could I feel I could create the country on my own terms, the old world's terms meeting the American terms, a place where the wheel never stopped turning and where my voice mattered? I'm tempted to put myself ahead of the curve: Abe Starker, Boy Wonder Who Sees the Record-Contract-Civil-Rights-Movement-Rimbaud-in-the-Village Future. That wouldn't be true, but I was a bundle of presentiments too. I wouldn't want to dismiss whatever vapors were in my head, because they're still there.

. . .

I got off a boat and looked around—
Fear looking back at me—
Found some rooms, a wife, a job—
Murdered my childhood country.

What I learned: That people want you to sign on the dotted line. That people want to sell you a share. That people have a scheme that could make a pile of money. That people have a surefire thing. That people want to know if you really mean what you say. That people would like to give you a break, cut you some slack, get to the point. That people wonder where you get your ideas from. That people think you should have stopped a while ago. That you're just repeating yourself. That people tell you how you've been lucky and they've been unlucky, but if they'd have been lucky they would have been better than you. That people know someone who used to know you. That people come from a small town like the one you come from. That people say they identify with you but they wouldn't want to be you. That people ask if you believe in God. That people say, "nothing personal," and then say something personal. That people have expectations you don't meet. That people think the critics are right but not right all the time. That people need a chance. That people need a second chance. That people wonder how you got where you are. That people think you're shorter than they thought you were. That people tell you that you haven't done your share politically. That you haven't used your influence correctly. That you still could make a difference, though. If you listened.

You could get weary from people's thoughts. You could wear out on unasked-for advice. You could wonder if there always were fans or, worse, people who make a point of telling you they're not fans, who write long letters explaining why you are a fraud, an imposter, a no-talent jerk who can't sing a note and stole all his songs. Your fans can come up to you anywhere and start talking as if they know you. They have a theory about you. They have suggestions for you: just suggestions, nothing you have to do, but suggestions that might make sense. They're not all wrong—a different key or tuning or chord—who knows? I'm swimming in the sea of unknowing and they think I know something. I've followed my nose, my heart, my head, my belly, and my prick: The order has varied.

I'm me and you're you, I want to say, and let's leave it at that; except it's not that simple, and both of us know it. There's that weird, unseen bridge between us. I've spent many nights sitting and writing songs, and they've spent many nights listening to them. We match up but we don't. As much as I've tried to slot myself into roles—musicianer, minstrel, balladeer, rock 'n' roller—my metaphors have leaked out. I've been a fugitive from everywhere, but there I've been, up on the stage, sharing my dubious self, singing again about the glass moon of time.

One of the revelations along the way is that I haven't been the only fugitive. That's why there are bands and jams and sitting in and hanging out. The musical wire goes in every direction all over the planet. I suspect because it can't be articulated, because music is the articulation in its own particular way that this thread among the people who make music is unspoken. For sure, there's a common story—the one about a world that doesn't put music first and you being a person who does put music first. "For guys who are so harmonic, you guys are all dissonant," one of the women I was with used to say. She was right. Going off the tracks comes naturally. You take the basic frustration of your caring and multiply that by indifference and you get a large, unhappy number. Yet the sounds sustain you. When they don't, you can fall through some serious cracks. Your reality's been unreal.

Poets say that poetry is essential as bread, but not many people are poets. People manage to get along fine without poetry. They confine their wonder to Wonder Bread, thank you. I get it; but if life doesn't go farther than our next meal, that's not very far. The way the songs have been essential to me—my ballast and astute pleasure—makes me feel sometimes that the words in the songs aren't really English, that they make up a different language, one that comes from one lost feeling embracing another. More is happening than I ever know what to do with, which means I'm living a life on top of or beside or within my regular days. Actually, I have no regular days, so I take that back. The days are shot through with the writing, which is episodic but always hovering. People press a button on a machine and start listening, but whatever led up to the songs and the random and not-random tissue of imagination that abides and leaps and disappears and reappears is nowhere to be seen. A lot of the questions the interviewers ask—the ones that try to get at my head rather than what guitar I use—are, in that way, very beside the point. We're talking about tatters fluttering in a coming-from-all-directions wind.

Though I've seemed to the journalists elliptical and oblique, I've tried to answer the questions. What they don't often get is how shadowy the endeavor is. The songs may seem solid, but the person who made the songs is not. No one, to my way of thinking, is solid, but we act that way because we keep answering to the same name. You could say the songs are about that conflict: our trying to be solid and all the not-solid stuff that goes with life, beginning with love. How could I not be amused at the questions trying to pin down influences and categories? I never bought into the normal course of the days. It wasn't courage. I wouldn't have known how.

◦ ◦ ◦

> Like God to Job, the dick talked sharp—
> Where'd you leave your face?
> I knew that spiel, skipped town, mailed it in—
> Entered a fugitive state.

Like many kids when I was growing up and the moon was far away, I read science fiction. I remember a book cover where a guy in a space suit was falling—white stars and blackness around him. I haven't been out in the far reaches of the universe, but I've been falling for a lifetime into the depth of women, a sort of cosmic well. I don't mean that women are inherently deeper than men. I mean that for me there's the gravitational pull into what's different and seems understandable but isn't, the language that's held in common but echoes in unexpected directions. The songs about saying goodbye outnumber the songs about saying hello.

When I put down the science fiction and turned on the radio, there were the women. They had on a red dress and diamond rings and could do the Birdland all night long. What was the "Birdland"? Definitely far from rural Minnesota and definitely sexy. I wanted to meet those women. I wanted a piece of that throbbing musical wildness. You listened to Ray Charles and felt how these women were queens, as regal as they were hot. They could make you fall on your face or raise you up to Birdland heaven—wherever that was.

To be ever falling is an uncanny feeling. You're going about your days, reporting for duty, as my dad would have said, even if my duty has been sketchy. At the same time a siren is calling—a very sweet sound. You aren't in control in the way you'd like to think you are. You could think of Ulysses and how he had to stop up his crew's ears so they wouldn't hear. Since I'm a musician, that feels like the worst fate—not to hear. And impossible, because every songwriter has been right about using the word "falling" when love comes on. Yet it's not just love. It's the jolt of how electric the field is and how so much of each day hides that electricity away. Except that it's not like putting a toy in a chest or a feeling into a cliché. Who are we kidding?

So I've written songs in which one word picture falls into another: the song about the woman who got what was coming to her on account of her pride and the one about the woman who ignored love and the one about the woman who couldn't bear with love and the one about the woman who left and came back and left again. It's a long list. The unhappy amusement is that I've lived each of them.

And there's the turning of the tables: the man who couldn't be bothered about love and the man who misrepresented love and the man who wanted thanks for his love and the man who feigned love when what he wanted was sex. If love were a mirror, I couldn't bear to look into it.

This tangle has left me with scars and tunes and—no matter what—keen remembrances. As every twelve-year-old straight guy intuits, every female body is a more than adequate version of heaven. When I first saw a Modigliani painting, I got weak. He painted what I had been trying to sing about. And even though the painting is a surface, he got the depth, the hard rapture of the reality. He got the look in the woman's eye, which isn't some bullshit seduction but the quiet cataclysm of attraction and awareness of attraction. For him, there was no getting away from women, nor would he want to. The entanglements came later. The paintings reside in the pure here-I-am energy.

Modigliani was a Jew who seemed to become another man when he moved to Paris and began making his art. Maybe he knew he was going to die soon. Maybe he had to become someone else to do the paintings he needed to do. He probably knew that no one would particularly understand what he was up to, that after the erotic charge, people would comment on how the women's necks were too long and walk away to look at someone who got the necks right. That's how art works for most people—fill in the blanks correctly so people can nod as if they knew all along what every mystery was about.

He knew what the falling was and devoted his life to that falling. It's nothing against the women I've known to say that I never knew a woman like the great Russian poet Anna Akhmatova, with whom he had an affair. He and she, Amadeo and Anna, that must have been heady yet crazily physical—two living myths coming together, poetic magnets. You don't envy someone's loves, though. You seek your own; they seek you. I've kept mine private because they're not anyone's business. The celebrity racket reduces love to a headline, as if love could be a news item in two columns, as if the falling weren't the hungry, beyond-words truth.

. . .

Love stood in the doorway watching—
I held my partial breath—
The moment skittered—marbles on ice—
Like time denying death.

When I first came to New York City, I lived here and there, sleeping on couches, sometimes on the floor with my overcoat as a blanket and bed. In their offhand ways, people were open and welcoming. The city, or at least downtown, was still soft, not overrun by money and bustle, not so full of itself, not corporate but still personal—people living their disorganized, life-size lives. People like me came to the city as seekers, people without a career in any regular sense. What I wanted to do wasn't taught in any college or sold by any company. I needed to be among like-minded people who could listen, people I could share my love of music with, people I could learn from. I knew about the people playing in Washington Square. I knew about the clubs where you played for tips. Folk music was made up, but the scene was real. If I was going to get noticed, New York was the place.

There was more to it than getting noticed. There was my starting to grow up, starting to realize how much more there was to the world than the town I grew up in. I knew that—that's why I left—but that's not the same as living it. My couple of months in Chicago, where I stayed with a guy who knew a guy from my town, was a way station on the road to New York, a sort of catching my breath before moving on. Chicago belonged to the Midwest, the ocean of land. New York was the East—older and more settled and more aware—but also a little planet that spun on its own axis. Greenwich Village had been attracting people from elsewhere for decades. I didn't know all the stories about those people, but I knew history lay under my boot heels when I first started walking around, looking at the brick buildings, climbing five flights of stairs, and finding my way among the crazy quilt of the downtown streets. I wouldn't admit it, because I was too occupied trying to be cool to admit anything, but I was thrilled. I could have sent a postcard home but didn't.

Meeting people was crazy. Everyone was like a dog sniffing another dog: Who are you? I veered between sincerity and distance. I wanted to meet everyone and take in everything. I wanted to make people know who I was when I didn't know myself who I was. I wanted to make my mark but had no idea what my mark might be. I was there, though, walking the sidewalks and telling people if they wanted to know what a cold winter was they should check out northern Minnesota. I felt someone was calling my name even as I was losing my name. I looked at people looking at me. No more time in front of mirrors: That was for preparing; that was the past. In New York I was on the stage and better act that way.

Some days I could feel how much of an act I was, but other times I couldn't do much more than blurt and spurt, raw innocence posing as knowledge. It pains me to look back, not out of shame—no one was a saint that I ran into—but the bad manners of me, how much I put myself onto other people, how I didn't know any better and didn't want to know any better. Some people were amused; some were put off; but some people let me in for more than the floor space and a bowl of cereal. Those people were precious. I lacked the wit to tell them that. I took them for granted as if I had their welcomes coming to me. When you're making yourself up, there is no map. The say-thanks manners my mother taught still applied and I used them, but the larger manners were beyond me. I sang about humanity but didn't understand how I was part of it.

I couldn't have put my heart out the way I did if I also didn't sneer. Contempt isn't a good friend, but he's a reliable one. He keeps you honest and dishonest at the same time, hard on others and soft on yourself. Fortunately, more than one woman stepped forward and told me how I was my own enemy.

Sometimes, I even listened to them. Not that I became modest.
I was too much on fire, but I started to see—lying in bed and
talking with a woman after sex, feeling awake and drowsy at
the same time, sated yet alert—how I wasn't the summit of anything and didn't have to be. A woman has another life waiting
inside her, which gives a woman a double mind a man doesn't
have. I was going to put Eve in more than one song.

Some people, mostly guys, sneered back. Where do you
come from, buddy, and what do you know, and are you doing
it at my expense? We were competing for literally very small
change, but that never held us back. What were we without our
jealousy? Whatever we were aiming for must have been worth-
while if we were willing to step over one another to get there.

With women the competition was subtler. Any social
moment contained lights and shadows that I knew nothing
about. Any moment could be unraveled in the words that
came easily to their lips: "You're just a boy, Abe." I felt, as I sat
at tables in the little downtown cafes, like a bale of hay, the
true Midwestern yokel. Yet a sideways glance from me could
set a woman crying. I despised myself for that. I reveled in it.

. . .

Thought about each brick in the wall—
Moved from dream to dream—
Vision erupting, abrupt, unkempt—
My days fell in between.

I didn't want to be a story the way Garrett Gray, the reigning
downtown folksinger, was a story: how he knew so many

songs, how he had bummed around the country, how he was the real thing. I met him. He did know hundreds of songs. He had bummed around. He let you know it too, but whether he'd been arrested in Tulsa, Oklahoma, for vagrancy or not, I didn't want to become that story, the story of the genius of my events. If there was any genius, it was going to have to be imagination.

When I was growing up, I heard stories all around me: people talking about themselves and what happened here and there, embellishing but diminishing their lives. That sounds harsh, but I felt as if words made a sort of funnel: What was large and all-over-the-place, like all the land that comprised the nation, became narrow. There was a resignation there, not to fate, because Americans are about possibility, but about an inevitable shrinkage, how a choice here and a choice there made a life. How that was it—done.

"And who are you, Abe, to protest?" my father, that one-man chorus of there's-work-to-do perseverance, might have said. In his way, he did say that, pointing out that I had to live before I knew anything. That was my point, though. People lived, but I wasn't sure what they learned. They learned so they could confirm their notions. They seemed more closed than open, more safe than discovered, looking for a haven or a reason. Nothing beckoned to them.

That seemed sad, although I kept the feeling to myself— or better, I let the feeling out in the songs. At the least, other people's songs that went into my songs taught me that not everyone knew the same things. The nation's genius, and reason for anything like real patriotism, was its immensity and diversity. In New York, where there were men like Garrett, who had made a point of rambling, there were also men like Steve Roster, who never went much beyond Bleecker Street but had hundreds upon hundreds of records. You could ramble in your head too. You didn't have to belong to anything if you didn't want to.

I hung out with both those guys. As the first among equals, Garrett was wary but assumed the mantle of open-road, been-there authenticity. He operated via casual one-ups. He was older; I was younger. He'd lived; I hadn't. I was the puppy chewing discarded shoes. When he told me a story about some gig or woman, he was throwing me a bone: "This is real life, Abe. You may get there and you may not." When they were together, Steve needled Garrett about his tales, about how you didn't have to be a human road atlas to be a musician. Steve was all about traditions and versions. As one of the guardians of the folk flame, he one-upped me too. I was some outlier who had little idea of what I was dealing with. In his fussy, cataloging way, he was right; but, as with Garrett, he thought I wanted to be like him. I didn't.

My pathless path came down to words. What I preferred to do with them was to not let them make up stories. In a song, this could happen and that could happen: Someone ran away on a horse or a train or in a car. Someone got into love or out of love. All well and good; the story for me, however, wasn't meant to be conclusive. The story was a way for the words to hitch a ride. The words pictured a mood or person or scene or drama. One of my interests was to undo stories, the way they meant to be so definitive, the way I grew up with:

Old So-and-So, he'll never change. Young So-and-So, he'll never change. Middle-Aged So-and-So, he'll never change. The repetition gets on your nerves, doesn't it? It got on mine. I knew there was a story to back up the declarations, complete with disappointment and a piece of old-fashioned bad luck. I vowed to follow the words to whatever lay on conclusion's other side.

That wasn't the promised land, but it was a place where my head could live and even thrive. When you go on a quest in plain view of other people, it's dicey. You're up on a stage to show people that you know what you're doing, not where you've wandered. But I've wandered intentionally. That's what artists do. Entertainers have a clear focus—do the gig and please the crowd. I respect that and I've done that, but the heart of my matter is unclear, no matter how many interviews I give. Things look clear when you look back: That was the album he went to Spain and lived with that woman; that was the album his wife left him; that was the album he got together with that great pedal steel guitar player. Looking back is like that: A story is bound to appear, a shape takes hold. You nod your head when the world tells you who you are and what you've done. You say polite words back or you don't. You sneer and spit and protest. Neither way matters. You're bound to be consumed and subsumed.

It bugged me when I was young and expected people to respect the artist in me. I learned. I wouldn't say the hard way. I got to make albums and play music. Recognition, though, is a thin street, given on the world's terms. Every original move is countered by the mass of what's taken for granted, what's expected, what's assumed, what's manageable. A whole parade of wearisome behaviors confronts the man up there with his guitar and not-the-world's-best voice. "Take a deep breath" isn't bad advice.

I could have stayed in a room and played my songs to the walls. Right this minute, some very talented souls are doing that. I didn't have to go out into the arena. That's true. The fuse that's been burning in me is the basic one: Connect. I've wanted people to hear me. Despite the sunglasses and affected cool, I've been eager. Seems only human. The story isn't what counts, but the impulse to write down the words and chords does count. You invite what's larger than you into the house and you honor that presence. Garrett and Steve did that too, but the words in their songs weren't as alive to them. For them the words already were decided, the grooves already channeled—a hopeful, tuneful drone. For me the words could add up to something very like a poem. They could surprise.

• • •

> Songs strung among the alleys and streets—
> You might bump into one—
> What do you say to the rising notes?
> No place safe to run.

I must have been in one of those pass-the-basket cafes when I met Sister Lou. She must have come up to me after I played for my twenty or so minutes, other people's songs but one or two of my own, and asked me who I was and what I was doing. She was nothing if not direct. I came to New York to make my head spin, to realize that my intimations were true about how many more people there were in the world. That wasn't a hard surmise to prove, but Sister Lou extended my intimations a great distance.

After talking with her some and going back to her place and having sex that was like nothing I'd ever experienced—I mean the sense of a woman's pleasure and my giving a woman that pleasure—she told me as we sat in bed smoking cigarettes that she was going to take advantage of me and that I'd enjoy that. She looked at me sideways, half-smiling and half-serious. Since she was "biracial," to use her term, she was comfortable with halves: They made more than a whole. I had no reason to doubt her, a woman who had taken on a name because her given name didn't "do me justice," who needed, as she put it, "something different." Here was someone making up her legend as she went along. I wanted to learn about that.

Sister Lou, or "Sister" as I came to call her, wasn't a musician. She called herself a "camp follower." "Those men in the wars needed women," she told me. "And for some women there is nothing like not knowing where your next male meal is coming from." She hung out in the clubs at night and worked as a secretary in midtown during the day. She saw no reason to cut herself off from the straight world. They made the rules and they cut the checks. Why pretend otherwise? What interested her was the nighttime, the personal hustle that went into downtown's random circuits.

She was older by five or so years, which was part of her allure—an experienced woman, not a girl. She was amused by me, my pretensions and my cover-ups, but she had a sense right away, right there meeting her in that cramped cellar where you barely had room to breathe, that I was after something. "You're an idealist," she announced a few days after we first met. "I studied philosophy in college, and you fit the role. That means you're likely to take some serious tumbles, Abe." She smiled indulgently. "Unless you listen to a woman of the world who knows how to walk the line." She paused. "I mean the race line, but also the sanity line."

In and out of bed, she read to me. She liked Dostoevsky and claimed no one ever understood people better than he did. She told me about how he was almost executed and how that freed something up in him so he didn't have to hold anything back. "Every one of us," she said, "is holding back, but Dostoevsky didn't. He'd seen his death for real. He must have tasted it." I'd barely heard who he was. She'd pick up *The Brothers Karamazov* or *Crime and Punishment* and start reading— the words a wave of intensity that seemed to have no end and no beginning. Then she'd drop the book and put her arms around me. "Do you know what to do with a woman, Abe?" she'd ask, her voice warm on my neck. "You can learn."

Maybe this seems like a joke, her veering between playful and earnest and my not-knowing-what-else-to-do willingness, the joke of once-upon-a-time American bohemia trying to live on Dostoevsky, acoustic guitars, and fornication. We say something is a time in life, typically when we are looking back and relegating that time to the dustbin of the impractical or nostalgia. In her quiet moments, Sister liked to muse about how she'd wound up in the skin she'd wound up in, something that amounted to more than a time in life. She'd run a finger along my body as we lay in bed. "Bet you take your skin for granted," she said, shrewd sadness in her voice. "That's why you can develop all this philosophical collateral you're carrying around. That's why your songs can be lively and unhappy at the same time. You don't have to think twice, and when you do, you feel it does some good. Even though you're intense, you still have some of that white blandness about you." She'd laugh her seen-too-much laugh. "You haven't been dipped in the ineradicable solution."

I'd nod as if I knew something. I felt as if we were crossing a mine field, and then I started to feel how a metaphor could be real—how when I was with her sometimes in public, in a club or café, and someone would walk by and look at her the tiniest bit beyond how you regularly look at a stranger and then a tiny bit more at me and then walk on. Nothing blew up, but every moment was charged in that uncertain, what-is-this way. And that, as Sister liked to remind me, was every day. "See my skin," she would say; "see the shards, slivers, splinters. Words you might put into a song."

The word "love" never appeared. I tried out a few songs on Sister, and she was kind about my intentions—"accept that you're a good Jewish boy"—but merciless about the details. "You're trying too hard to not make sense" was one of her favorite remarks. What she got was how much the songs counted, no matter how, when I was with Garrett or Bob, I'd try to be just one of the guys: "Yeah, I write a song every now and then, no big thing." Sister let me say out loud to one person, "This is a real big thing. For me there's nothing bigger." Saying that to her felt better than good. Saying that was what they call "coming out" these days.

One day on the street, I ran into a guy who lived in her building on Second Street. "Did you hear about Sister Lou?" he asked. I cringed as if I could hide in the jacket I had on. "She split. The West Coast, I think. Or maybe Mexico. I heard it secondhand, but she's gone." He waved a hand. "Far from here, man." He stopped waving. "And far from you, Abe." "Thanks, man," I said. "Good to know." I went on to whatever purpose I was heading toward, not surprised but feeling twisted up inside like something was gone that, even though I was young, would never come back. Not some months of life, but a woman. Someone who let me into her body but kept her soul at a safe distance. "I'm the teacher, Abe," she would say. "You can imagine plenty, but you can't imagine me." Years and years later I got a postcard from her. "You made it. I knew it. Must be boring. Sister Lou."

. . .

Poetry books all over—a cat
Who perched atop cupboards—
Sighs for lost time—sex-grunts
For the tongue beyond words.

Days in Greenwich Village I spent gobbling up records; nights I spent playing and listening to others play. Gradually I worked my way up the list on the bill; gradually I made enough money to not be cadging money. The Village was my university, where my classes consisted of sitting on lumpy sofas and rickety chairs while cats—calico, Siamese, tuxedo—made themselves comfortable on my lap and learning how Uncle Dave Macon played the banjo and what a cowboy song really was and how Blind Lemon Jefferson got that guitar tone. What might have seemed arcane to others—Uncle Dave Who and Blind Lemon What—made for my natural syllabus.

I started to be inside the music and not outside it. Every artist understands how this works, how there comes a time when you begin to feel how you are part of what you are learning and how it makes sense to you, a sense that is yours and not the teacher's. There wasn't any special, overpowering moment when that happened. When I listened to the records or heard guys play, I was taking something into me that was constructing me just as I was constructing myself—Abe Runyan, not Abe Starker. The name difference might not have seemed a big deal. Any way you cut it I was, as Sister Lou reminded me, a Jew, but I was removing myself from my history. I was taking myself home to my truest place—my imagination. How much of a home that would be, I would have to find out. When someone called out "Hey, Runyan" on the street, I looked around. Where was he?

What I was trying to imagine over the course of those New York months that became years and that exhilarated and scared me was a world in which people took my songs to heart. What I was trying to feel was that the audiences that I encountered, who could be anywhere from indifferent to enthusiastic, could be my audience, that they could listen to me for the sake of me and not just for something to do on a Friday night. And

I was trying to feel that my songs could take aim at them, that they were people around my age who had lived in the nation where I had grown up and dealt with the same stuff, whether it was air raid drills or Elvis or desegregation or Chevrolets or wondering what Dwight Eisenhower had to say to them. But the songs had to be personal at the same time. I wasn't interested in writing songs the way some guys would pick a topic and write a song. The first and last thing was that a song was made up. That meant that what was sad might turn out funny and what was funny might turn out sad, and I had to be good with that and not force it.

When I started putting my songs out to people in public, I did the usual downplaying, the this-is-just-something-I-wrote-the-other-day approach. It took me a while before I could really sing them. At the beginning I more or less mumbled them. I didn't so much lack confidence as I had a hard time feeling that what was happening was actually happening. I was in my head so much that even when people were right there in front of me, I didn't quite take that in. When the so-called underground cartoons came along in the '60s, I got them right off because they captured that sense of being in a separate reality. What happened, though, was that people started to share their separate realities. I stopped mumbling and started singing.

When people applauded one of my songs, when I could tell they were listening, when they crossed the line between yeah-I-know-that-ballad to who-is-this-guy, I felt a glimmer. I kept the glimmer to myself. There was the usual amount of backbiting around me. Garrett wasn't about to be dethroned as the reigning folk eminence. That was fine with me. I was coming in through another door. If you change the game's terms, it becomes a different game.

When you look back, things seem programmatic—Abe on his musical mission—but I know they weren't. I spent my share of time learning what marijuana was and how much booze I could drink and still find the bathroom. There was what you might call communal rollicking. We needed one another, and as much as I was trying to find myself and distinguish myself, I needed everybody around me. I could never have believed in myself if there hadn't been those people around me who liked to play the songs and listen to the songs and talk about the songs and drink wine and eat spaghetti and argue politics and baseball. The word "community" gets thrown around in the United States because community is so sketchy here with all these different people, each one searching out his or her pathway; but for a time there was a community there among the folksingers—or at least a tribe.

That scene didn't last, but that doesn't diminish its importance. Anytime something happens when people come together about something that is imaginative in a good way— not about an army or making more money—but something that is going to feed people's spirits, I'd count that as a serious plus. Did people take advantage of other people? Yes. Did I? Yes. Some of the small change of hurt feelings wasn't so small, but I had my eye on a near yet faraway prize. What started to dawn on me in New York was that the pie could be as large as my head could make it. There was no limit. And I could push on all sides—expand what a song could be while making fun of myself, while letting the song be as earnest or wistful or off-the-wall as I wanted it to be. I didn't have to take out a license to go into the revelation business.

• • •

Buildings were higher, sky was less—
Night was never that dark—
How did this welter come to be?
When did Sense disembark?

Back then the Village was a village. People in and around the scene knew one another. So when one morning in the Italian cafe I liked to hang out in a friend of a friend came up to me and shoved a newspaper in my face, I wasn't taken aback. There were many friends of friends who were full of announcements and pronouncements. What she showed me was a review of my gig the night before. The main act had been some bluegrass players—real good pickers. I was the opening act. I'd played some standards, but I'd played some of my songs—the goofy one about World War Two and a Half, the one about a miner's wife, the one about a woman leaving town and not telling anyone, the one about the sky above the land where I grew up, and a real new one about how you couldn't judge people by the color of their skin. The reviewer liked my songs.

I sat there and read it again. I laughed and smiled. The woman who showed me the piece began talking about how important it was to get this kind of notice, how plenty of people wished they could get such a notice. I sat there and listened to her, but I wasn't listening. I felt apart from myself, as if I were watching myself: Here's Abe being "discovered." And where was Abe before that? He got up that morning and wondered whether he had the money to get a new guitar he'd been coveting, and he noticed he'd forgotten to buy more toilet paper and he remembered someone who still owed him five bucks and probably wouldn't pay it back. He walked down the flights of stairs to the street and thought about how much he needed a cup of espresso. He'd sat there with that cup not waiting for anything.

I excused myself after thanking the woman, Susan was her name, and went for a walk. I headed over toward the Hudson. I didn't so much need to clear my head as find my head. What did the words mean? You aim for something, but you don't know what it really is you're aiming at until you get there. Then you still don't know, because other people's aims are in there too. The reviewer said I was a "fresh talent." I had to wonder. Would he have called Lead Belly that when he first heard him? Or Bessie Smith? Their worlds didn't run that way. As Sister Lou pointed out to me, I had my advantages. I had my rough edges too. So I was surprised to see those words in the paper, because I suspected the reviewer was familiar with the categories and how the categories came before the person.

But I was whoever I was, and I had to go with that. As I walked along the streets toward the docks, I thought of nothing so much as how I wanted to write more songs, and knew I would write more songs. People would say what they would say, but the skein of my circumstances was my particular skein. I thought of the movie *Citizen Kane* and how it was about someone who became tremendously famous and pow-erful but who still was the sum of his childhood and grow-ing-up circumstances. The fame was like a crust over him, and I could see in the movie how easy it was for the crust to take over, for the person to become the exterior. What was in there, though, was still in there.

It seemed I should be running around crowing to people about what the reviewer had written, but that wouldn't have been cool. Any player would have thought, "Why did he notice Abe and not me?" That would have been understandable. There were guys who played much better than I played and sang better than I sang. I'd come from nowhere, and here was this review saying I was somewhere. How did that happen?

I got to the piers and looked at the ships and the river. Growing up where I grew up, I felt almost shocked when I saw the river and thought how the ocean was so near. I stood there for a time, staring at the water and feeling the breeze on my face. I felt not so much full of my life as emptied out. I felt not so much inclined to look to the future as to feel the wisps of all the days before. I felt something clear in me, something complete. Someone had nodded in my direction—a stranger. Gulls flapped around above me—living their lives. I wanted to holler for the sake of hollering. I did.

I turned away and headed back to my apartment, to the streets I had come to know and to the gig I was playing that night. I was going to hear from people about the words in the paper, and I was going to nod and smile and act as if it was no big thing—even though we knew it was a big thing, getting noticed. Each of us up on those stages had our dreams. The dreams came from records and books and posters and movies, but most of all from other lives that somehow had penetrated our lives. I remembered reading plays in high school and how they were divided into scenes and acts. I'd reached the end of an act. Maybe people would not only start to look at me a little differently but listen a little differently. Maybe I would feel the words in my songs in a way I hadn't felt them before, a little crisper, a little surer. No wonder "maybe" was one of my favorite words. I didn't need a headline to tell me that nothing could be predicted but everything mattered. I was sure of that, how my age didn't enter into it. My heart had been tested by music. I'd been true.

CPSIA information can be obtained
at www.ICGtesting.com
Printed in the USA
FSHW011547240720
72244FS